*What if everywhere you've ever been,
has an unknown 'world' living below it?
Unknown that is to most, but not to all…*

Chapter 1

A Move Too Far?

Sion Roberts of Staffordshire was not moving to rural Wales and that was the end of it!

It was the last week of July, school had finished for the summer, but this was not going to be a normal summer for Sion. The day was here, already. That day. The day he had dreaded, since first hearing those words.

"You're going to love the new house, Sion."

He wasn't going to love it. He was sure of that. He was going to hate it. He was even surer of that. Using his unrivalled selective hearing skills, Sion sat cross-legged on the floor of his now bare room, ignoring the calls from his ever frantic mother. He wasn't going anywhere. They were welcome to go without him, he'd be fine, he thought.

Sion sat, rocking slightly, muttering moderately rude thoughts about his parents, when suddenly, a very large and very sweaty, red-faced man appeared in the doorway. Sion was startled, not just by the look of this unfamiliar person, but more by the fact that a man of this stature, had managed to get all the way up the stairs to the bedroom door, without Sion noticing.

"Yer right mate?" The stranger asked.

Stammering slightly and rubbing his nose, as he did when nervous, Sion responded.

"Er, yeah ta, I'm fine. Er, thanks."

"It's just yer all that's left 'ere now, so we wouldn't want yer to be 'ere on yer own, like. Overnight. Or longer. Would we? Eh?"

Sion shrugged and grunted one of those teenage grunts that attempts to resemble 'I don't know', but to the untrained ear, just sounds like a regular grunt.

"Come on lad," the stranger continued. "You do really need to come down now. I know you're feeling down, I can see that. But, it won't be all bad, you'll see. I know the area yer going to. Beautiful place. Lots to explore for a lad like you."

He now sounded softer. More friendly. Sion glanced up at him and after it had been wiped on an already grubby vest, took hold of the gargantuan hand being offered to him. For a split second, as he was thrust to his feet, Sion thought his arm had been pulled clean out of its socket. He looked up from the hand of the stranger to his flushed, prickly face. Sion noticed the tattoo on the man's neck. Small and barely visible amongst the large quantities of flesh. A symbol of sorts, a bit like a dart board but with fewer segments. Some segments were coloured in a dark red colour and others with a greenish brown.

"Tarquin's the name. And who might you be?"

"I'm Sion. Sorry to be rude, but you don't look much like a Tarquin," Sion replied in a slightly apprehensive fashion.

"Er, no. Yer right. I don't. Me mates call me Quinny. You can too if you like. Me mum. God rest her soul, had delusions of grandeur. She thought that if she gave us posh names, like Lords and Ladies, then I'd become rich and famous. She 'ad some funny ideas. Bless 'er."

Without realising what he was doing, Sion plodded down the narrow staircase behind Tarquin. He turned briefly for one last glance at the door of his room, still with its Liverpool FC stickers plastered all over it. He noticed the Peppa Pig sticker on the bottom right corner. His younger sister had stuck it there last a few years ago. He was really annoyed at the time, but right now, he wished he could keep the door, with all its stickers. Even the bright pink Peppa Pig one.

As he reached the bottom step, he was greeted by his father. A generally quiet man, he put his arm over Sion's shoulder and led him through the front door, towards the car.

"Let me know if you need help getting your belt sorted, will you? You're a bit tightly packed in there."

Sion fiddled about and clicked his seatbelt shut.

At the end of the drive, half blocking the busy road, Tarquin was hauling himself into the driver's seat of the removal van. Sion began thinking about how they'd get Tarquin into their car if he'd been travelling with them. He giggled to himself at the image in his head. A family of four pushing a man the size of a small island into the back of a loaded Vauxhall Corsa!

Sion heard the beep from the removal van, as it pulled out onto the main road. Dad waved and got into the car.

"Just waiting for your mum," Dad remarked wearily. "She's just giving the house one last look over. Again. Make sure we've got everything."

Sion's sister Gwen was engrossed in an episode of Friends; tablet on her lap, luminous pink headphones balanced on her plaited hair. Sion hated those shows. The accents, the sets and most of all, being told by a computerised noise when to laugh. Sion didn't recall a time that he'd ever actually seen his sister laugh when watching them. Maybe they're magic? Maybe you are put into some kind of trance? As he pondered this thought, his mum came out of the house, locked the door, posted the key back through the letterbox and hurried over towards the car, arms laden with random objects. There seemed to be something belonging to everyone, even the dog. She handed Sion a miniature soldier figure with no head and a rather flat Hot Wheels Jeep with two wheels missing. He looked down at them before carefully depositing them onto the car floor. It was clear that one of the items recovered had been a toy belonging to Albert, as high pitched squeaks were now coming from the car boot.

Albert was a giant dog, literally, a giant dog. Albert was a Great Dane. A truly magnificent animal who from a distance resembled a small dappled horse and not a family dog. How on earth Sion's dad had managed to get him into the car, was a miracle! He only just went in on a regular trip out, but today with everything else, his presence in the car was like a new Wonder of the World. Despite his colossal size, Albert, like most Great Danes, was a gentle giant. Soft as butter. Innocent as a lamb. Daft as a brush. The only risk you took when greeting Albert, was being licked to death. And boy could this dog lick! His foot-long tongue was a mixture of sandpaper and slug. He meant well, but it could be a horrifying experience if Albert did manage to lick you, particularly if it was your face!

As the car pulled out from the driveway and onto the main road, Sion chose not to look back. He chose to look down. He stared at the two broken toys that he'd dropped into the foot well. A tear slowly made its way down his cheek. He cautiously wiped it away with one finger, ensuring that Gwen was blissfully unaware of her older brother's show of emotion. She'd be highly amused if she saw him cry. It'd give her bribing ammunition for years to come.

Sion began to gaze out of the window at the flat, green countryside whizzing by. Occasionally he'd spot a cow or tractor or section of canal, but mostly fields. Field after field. With earphones securely back in his ears, Sion allowed the journey to swallow him up. He'd finally given up his meagre protest.

Chapter 2

Sion

Sion Samuel Godfrey Roberts was thirteen years and five months old. His parents had not been able to choose between two great-grandfathers for his middle name, so had settled on both. Throughout school, in England, his friends had nicknamed him 'Zion', due to their insistence that his name was spelt incorrectly. Sion always found this a bit hypocritical, considering that one of his friends had a bother with the same name, spelt S E A N.

Softly spoken, often shy and keen on his own space, Sion was the polar opposite to his sister, Gwen. He liked to keep himself to himself, always had done. He could spend hours creating Lego masterpieces, reading comics, drawing fantastical characters or just listening to music. That was another thing that Sion did differently. He had never had much time for chart pop or listening to something because it was popular at school. He liked music from the 80s and 90s; 'Britpop', 'grunge' and 'indie' acts. He loved Nirvana, Radiohead and Pixies, not to mention Doves, Nick Cave and Stone Roses. He'd had a record player for his last birthday, it was his pride and joy. He hoped to add to his record collection, as time went on, but it currently only stood at two; Hotel California by The Eagles and Strangeways, Here We Come by The Smiths. Both of which his dad had picked up in a charity shop for him. To be fair, they were both excellent and Sion could already sing along to the majority of tracks, without error. Girlfriend in a Coma from the latter, being his favourite, as his mother hated the lyrics. His friends called it all 'Sion's death music', as they claimed it was all 'beyond depressing'. But Sion, he loved the guitars and the angst, the often angry lyrics, set against ear-splitting riffs. He actually found it all strangely uplifting and more to the point, he couldn't give a monkeys what his friends thought. He might be quiet, but if Sion had an opinion, he'd make it known. Despite this, he was rarely a pain for his parents. He just got on with life and did as he was asked, within reason. He wasn't a fussy eater, unlike Gwen. He helped with jobs, unlike Gwen and seldom gave backchat, very unlike Gwen. Not being a fussy eater doesn't necessarily mean that you eat regular meals at all times though. Sion was well known for his unusual combinations, when sorting his own snacks. Creations frequently involved his beloved Marmite (which he would eat on a spoon from the jar, if the mood took him), but if he was in need of a fruit boost, he'd swap milk for orange juice on his cereal. This would always result in anyone present making vomit sound effects and pulling gag-reflex faces at his bowl. This pleased him, on every occasion. The most memorable occasion had been at his friend James' home, during a sleepover. James' mother had been so taken aback by Sion's breakfast choice, she'd fallen over their diminutive bichon-frise and sent its kibble, cascading across the pristine kitchen units!

Moving from his home in the Midlands to an old, detached house in the wilderness of Wales, had not been his choice, but in true Sion style, he'd get on with it. It was what it was. No amount of temper tantrums or teenage grumblings would alter the fact that he and his family were now residents of a (difficult to pronounce) village in the heart of Eryri. He would be making the most of his isolated lifestyle and was secretly looking forward to exploring the varied landscape that would now surround him.

Chapter 3

Is Adventure There?

21:42. Sion checked his watch as the handbrake creaked. Including a pit stop at a service station somewhere on the Cheshire/Wales border, it had taken three hours and forty-seven minutes to arrive. Arrive home. Sion didn't yet consider it home, but he knew that he would have to accept it sooner or later.

Albert made the unsuitably small Corsa shake, as he pestered to stretch his oversized canine limbs. Once the boot door opened, he did at least twelve laps of the car before Sion's mum finally attached a lead. Her heels leaving long marks in the gravel where Albert briefly dragged her.

A silence descended on the family, as the four of them stood, very still, taking in the view from the driveway. It was quiet. Very quiet. Sounds were few. They ranged from distant sheep to brief bird sounds, an owl maybe. Slowly flowing water to the dull tones of a faraway plane. Even as night fell, the view was, to all intents and purposes, spectacular. Several mountain peaks, countless waterfalls and sheep. A great deal of sheep. Sion decided, at that very moment, that if life was going to be good here, he was going to need to explore these hills. Every last inch of them. Possibly, with Albert in tow. Within seconds of that thought, Sion had chosen his first exploration. Within a clear visual distance of the house, a cave-like hollow appeared to him. The more he looked, the less he saw. It was settled, first thing tomorrow, he was going to investigate the mysterious gap in the mountain opposite the house.

Chapter 4

Gwen

In contrast to her brother, ten year old Gwen was volatile, argumentative and attention-seeking. It was a good job that Sion was so calm in comparison, as Gwen demanded at least ninety percent of their parents' attention. That's not to say that she was all bad; she had a caring and compassionate side, but that was mostly shared with animals or trees. Gwen was a self-confessed 'tree-hugger'; she liked to name them too, generally with male, human names. She had a few favourite trees near their old house (Jim, Ross and Joey) and it was a tearful few hours when she said her goodbyes to them. Their mother had decided not to divulge that the HS2 route was dangerously close by and that the trees in question may not be there much longer anyway. On arrival at the new house, Gwen had been thrilled by the mammoth sycamore in the garden, so much so, she'd leapt from the car in excitement, forgetting that she was attached to her tablet. She could still watch Friends with the cracked screen, but it was a bit of a nuisance.

Another difference between the siblings was their diet. Gwen was fussy. She claimed to be vegetarian, but insisted that sausages and bacon (and chicken nuggets from McDonald's) didn't count. She only ate a minimal selection of vegetables and under no circumstances would she ever eat anything purple. She'd once chosen carrots as a bespoke accompaniment to a restaurant meal and had screamed unrelentingly when they appeared and were the posh purple carrots. If it'd been just their family, it wouldn't have been too bad, but it had been a treat from their father's boss and his wife, who both struggled to hide their mortified faces, during the hour long tantrum. Michelin Star restaurants are not often the setting for ear-splitting shrieks. Unsurprisingly, the Roberts family rarely visit posh restaurants anymore.

Gwen had no middle names, but she liked to conceal a secret about her name nonetheless. She was actually a Gwendoline, but only a selection of people knew this and she intended to keep it that way. As is to be expected, Sion regularly teased her about it and would quietly threaten to share the information, if Gwen was being particularly irritating. Most adults who heard it, loved her name and would coo about how pretty it was. Her peers were not so kind and would make jibes about her being tormented by dragons and other such fantasies.

It had come as a surprise to everyone in the Roberts family that Gwen had not put up much of a protest about moving, if any at all. In fact, she seemed to be seeing it as an adventure. Maybe once she knew that her friends would not be with her in September, realisation would hit, but for now at least, she was going with the flow of it all.

Chapter 5

Once or Again?

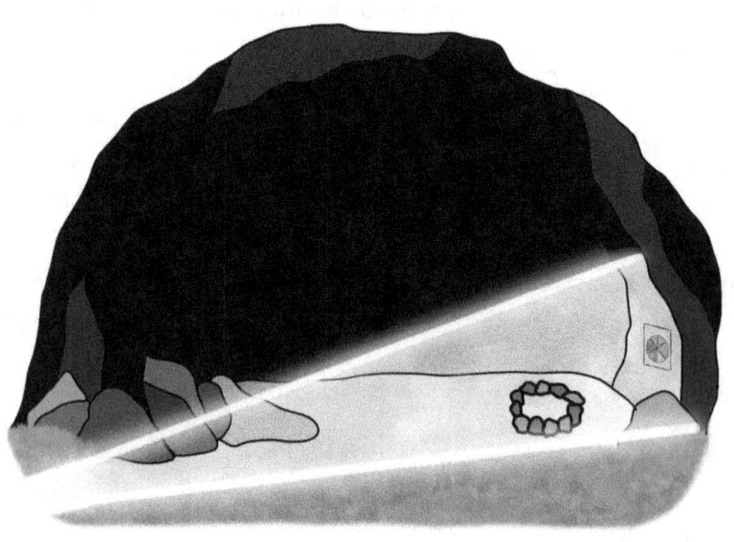

Considering the makeshift bed, constructed of books, boxes and towels, Sion had slept fairly well. The early morning sun had begun to seep into the room through the gap in the towels that were hanging from the ancient, rickety curtain rail. Sion lay still for a few minutes, staring at the ceiling, which had clearly been discoloured by decades of pipe smoke. He formed patterns and pictures in his mind with the amber swirls and blotches above him. Then he remembered, the cave! Sion sat upright and surveyed the room. His new bedroom. It was large, but oddly shaped. No wall was the same as another, in any way. The main window was huge, going almost from floor to ceiling and with twelve panes of glass, three of which were peculiarly distorted. Sion had not had a window that opened in this way before. It was his understanding that windows opened outwards, not up and down. He doubted if this one would open at all, it looked like it had been sealed shut for longer than he'd been alive! Maybe even longer than his parents! The second window was small, tiny in fact. So small that it almost seemed pointless. Why would a bedroom have a second window of this size? You couldn't even see through it without your head becoming stuck and there was no way of opening this one, at all. Sion was realising that there were going to be many things about this new/old house that he wouldn't understand.

Checking his watch, Sion padded gently across the bare floorboards, towards the larger window. It had a large ledge that was also a seat and an ottoman-style cupboard. Currently cushion-less, but still a great lookout post. Sion's mum had mentioned the evening before that she'd get a new cushion made for it soon.

Despite a little, lingering resentment for moving, Sion couldn't deny that the view from his new bedroom was an almighty one. Like a view on a postcard or a landscape painting, there was so much to see, it was impossible to take it all in. Sion sat silently, gazing out of the first floor window. Woodland, hills, distant mountains, a slow moving river, the top of a waterfall, sheep in their thousands and the cave. That cave! The cave he so desperately wanted to investigate. Last night, it had seemed far away, but now, in the morning light, it looked closer, much closer. In fact, it was probably no more than a ten minute walk away. From his window, Sion could see a footpath leading from outside of their house, through the adjacent field and across towards the cave. At least he hoped it was a cave. He'd be very disappointed if it turned out to be nothing but a crack in the rock. As he daydreamed, Sion's door creaked open.

"I'm doing bacon butties, do you want one, Sion?"

"Yes please. Got any eggs?" Sion replied, without turning around.

"Afraid not darling, just bacon. Red or brown sauce?"

"Red please," he muttered, without averting his gaze from the cave.

When the sound of his mother on the stairs quietened, Sion slipped off the window seat, picked up his clothes from the day before and put them back on. If you're off out into the wilderness, who needs clean clothes? Sion followed the smell of grilling bacon, out of his room, down the stairs and towards the kitchen. He was surprised to see that everyone else was already there, including Albert, who was making light work of his breakfast, pushing the metal bowl around the tiled floor as he attempted to lick up every last scrap. The sound always reminded Sion of small children playing musical instruments badly. Loud, unpredictable and annoying. 'It puts your teeth on edge," his mother would say. Not that he really understood what she meant.

While the other members of his family chatted about what the day ahead had in store for them, Sion mused over the cave. He thought about what he would say to his parents and if they'd actually let him go at all. Should he take Albert? Would he need a packed lunch? What if he fell or was injured? He had a mobile, but even so, an injury would surely jeopardise his chances of a return.

One by one, the Roberts family finished their breakfasts and left the kitchen, until it was just Sion, Albert and a large, hairy spider, which had startled Sion, scuttling across the unit, as he took his plate to the sink.

"I'm just going for a walk with Albert!" Sion hollered from the door.

He wasn't sure if he'd been heard, but it seemed like a good idea to just go, without a second shout. As the door banged shut, Sion heard his name being called from a window above him.

"Sion, where are you off to? Have you got bags for Albert?" Sion's mother enquired. "You mustn't leave his business for other people to step in, you know how big they are, people will just think they're cow pats!" she continued.

Sion rolled his eyes. "Yes mum, I've got poo bags and I'm not going far and I won't be long and I will be back for lunch and yes, I'm fine. Anything else?"

"No Sion! There's nothing else." Sion's mother snapped. "There's no need to be rude. I was just asking you a question. We only arrived yesterday. Are you sure you know where you're going? Can you give me an idea, just in case?"

Sion was unsure of how much information he wanted to give his mother. He did want to be safe, but he did not want to be followed.

"I saw a path in the field opposite, from my bedroom window. Can you see it? I'm just going to walk up that and back again, to look at the view," Sion lied. "I'll keep Albert on the lead. I just want to explore."

His mother glanced across to the field, from the upstairs window. Sion hoped that she'd not noticed the cave as she was bound to tell him not to go in it.

"Alright," she sighed. "Just please be careful and don't be out too long. Albert will be very excited by all the new smells, so you must keep a tight hold of that lead. Especially if you're picking up his business."

Sion sniggered. He'd always found it funny that his mother wouldn't say 'poo'. She also didn't like 'loo' or 'pants'. Sion continued to giggle to himself and he turned away from the house and began walking down the driveway and across to the beginning of the footpath.

He'd told a little lie to his mother about his walk and for his next trick, Sion had to get a sixty kilo dog, who was little under a metre tall, through a kissing gate! Albert had clearly understood Sion's quandary, as moments later, he leapt into the air and cleared the gate, like a thoroughbred horse in a steeplechase. Had it not been for the extendable lead, Sion would've shot through the air like a boy shaped comet. Pulling himself together and giving Albert a pat on the back, Sion studied the path and view in front of him. The path was not really a path, more a line of grass, as straight as a Roman road, running through the field. It just happened to be a slightly different shade of green to the rest of the grass. It wasn't well trodden, but was undoubtedly used from time to time, maybe even just by sheep. Sion's gaze moved from his feet, along the path and fixed on his destination.

The walk to the hill below the cave took a matter of minutes. Albert at plodding pace could cover quite a distance in no time at all. The second part of their walk was going to be a bit more hazardous, as the terrain changed from flat grassy path to steep scree covered hillside. Sion was confident that if he slipped, Albert's strength would help him, but he intended to complete this section on two feet, not fail miserably, on his bottom.

One methodical step at a time, Sion carefully made his way up. Not stopping to look up, or down, he kept his eyes firmly on where his feet were going next. To his surprise, Albert was not feeling confident on the loose rocks and stones. He was slipping frequently and despite his continued push upwards, Sion was debating with himself if he and Albert should turn back. Just as he began to mutter out loud, he saw it. There in front of him, as the ground in front of him flattened slightly, was the dark hole in the mountainside. It frightened him a little at first as he stared open mouthed. The gloom, the dripping, the remoteness. He could hear the sound of Albert panting next to him. By the side of the opening, there was a conveniently placed rock, just large and flat enough to make an excellent seat. Sion stumbled over to it and sat. His legs were like jelly and he was quite breathless. The hill had been strenuous, but the suddenness of his destination coming into view, had made him feel unexpectedly drained. From his seat, Sion could see his house, he could even see his own bedroom window. On closer inspection, he could see someone in the garden, his mother, he thought, but it was difficult to tell from such a height. He contemplated whistling or calling her, but he was certain that she'd assume he needed help and would instantly revert to her well-practised 'blind panic' mode. She was good at that, particularly when it was totally unnecessary, or so Sion thought anyway.

Chapter 6

What is Beyond the Gloom?

The feeling of serenity Sion had experienced, while studying the landscape around him, had wiped the purpose of his walk from his mind. Like the pop of a magician's trick, the cave behind him, returned to his thoughts. He turned and waited while his eyes became accustomed to the gloom in front of him. Albert had stirred too and was back on all fours. Sion was never quite sure what Albert could see, but it was obvious from his attentive sniffing that he knew there was somewhere to go in front of his nose. Sion ferreted about in his hoodie pocket for his torch. He imagined briefly, a scenario of forgetting it and shuddered at the thought. Just as Sion took a step forward, he smelled a familiar smell and not a pleasant one.

"Oh for the love of..." Sion began. Even without his mother, he knew to leave the end of that remark off. Once again, he went to the pocket at the front of his jumper and retrieved two black bags. Albert was a two bag type of dog! Heaving a little and holding his breath, Sion cleared up after his hound. Tying the bags up, he had an idea. If, just if, he was to become lost or stuck, he would need to be found. He placed the two filled bags on top of the stone he'd been sitting on. If he was being searched for, his parents would have an idea of his whereabouts. There wouldn't be many people here who carry poo bags weighing a similar weight to a packet of sugar!

Sion's torch wasn't the best, but illuminated enough of the cave for his slow steps. Albert wasn't pulling ahead, he was close to Sion's leg, so close that Sion almost tripped over him on more than one occasion. As they crept, it was impossible to see how far inside the hill the cave was going to go. It became cold. Sion shivered. He'd been sweating outside, after navigating the hillside in a large jumper, but now he was daydreaming about his winter coat and wishing he had his beanie hat on. A large drip of water landed on his head and ran down his cheek. It made him jump. He could feel that his feet were beginning to get wet too. Maybe he should stop and come back with a friend. What friend? He had none yet and he wasn't starting his new school for a month. Sion stopped walking. Even though he was now desperate to find out more, he was no fool. Today he'd focus on the entrance, see if he could see anything on the floor or walls. Next time he'd go farther, bring a better torch and more clothes, definitely more clothes. Sion turned and saw that the opening was closer to him than he'd thought; they hadn't gone far at all. He was amazed at how cold it had become so quickly. Sion liked the smell of the cave. It was a fresh, damp smell, like cold running water on a hot day. Sion moved his torch gradually, around the floor and onto the walls near the entrance. There was evidence of a small campfire. A circle of stones with tarred edges. He bent down and rubbed his fingers over the blackened stones. It was a fairly recent fire, Sion thought. Surely the damp and drips from above would have cleaned the stones, even if just a bit. As he ran his torch up the wall behind the fire, Sion could make out faint scribbles and marks. He stepped closer in an attempt to make something out. He could definitely see something, but his eyes were struggling in the poor light. Albert pulled at his arm slightly. The dog was right, he should be heading home. He'd said he wouldn't be long and he must have been gone for nearly an hour. If he worried his mother too much on his first walk, he'd not be allowed to go again without a chaperone. This he did not want. The cave was his find, his adventure. With that thought of defiance, Sion and Albert set off for home, grabbing the black bags and sliding down the scree on a mixture of feet and behind.

Chapter 7

Is That the Connection?

Over the next few days, Sion was unable to return to the cave. The weather had been horrendous. Horizontal rain and gale force winds that swirled in an unpredictable manner, knocking children from side to side. Sion's dad kept saying, "This weather is biblical!" And as he did so, he'd stand with his hands on his hips, slowly shaking his head, while looking out of a window. Even though the persistent stormy weather had postponed Sion's next cave trip, his mind had been on nothing else. He'd drawn himself a basic map of the route to the cave and what he knew about the inside so far. The one part of his visit he was most curious about was the evidence of other, recent visitors. The campfire and the wall markings. Every night, while he lay wide awake in bed, Sion thought about the scratches on the wall above the fire. They mostly seemed like nothing in particular; initials, little graffiti-style drawings, but the more he thought, the more he was sure that there had been a pattern. Something familiar or at least purposeful. He so desperately needed to go back and look again.

Then one evening, several days later, it came to him. It happened during dinner. Sion sat with his family around their large kitchen table. Dad had been into the town nearby to pick up a take-away. As Sion reached for the greasy paper bag of warm prawn crackers, his mother spoke,

"Oh, did I mention? Tarquin from the removal company rang today. He found that Allen key we're missing from the cupboard."

Sion stopped chewing. He sat motionless staring directly ahead at a bare wall. The talking at the table turned to a dull hum of nonsense in his head, like the teacher in Charlie Brown. That was it! But why? How? So as not to cause alarm or questioning, Sion finished the food on his plate, before muttering something about needing to wipe his greasy face and then leaving the table. No one seemed bothered, which he was very pleased about. He ran up to his room, pulled the sheets of paper and the pencil case out from under his bed and frantically began scribbling onto a new sheet. After a few minutes, Sion sat up from his hunched position and examined his work. He wasn't sure if it was quite right, but it was a start. Once again, he thought about how much he needed to go back to check the markings. Maybe he was wrong. Maybe he was overthinking. Sion tried to remember his time with Tarquin, it was only fifteen minutes, if that, but right now it seemed like the most important fifteen minutes in Sion's life. What had been said? Did he do or say anything significant? After several minutes of pacing his bedroom, "I know the village. Lots to explore!" Sion recalled out loud.

"Who are you talking to, Sion? Your imaginary friend?" Gwen had appeared in the doorway and was glaring at Sion with a look of smugness.

"No! Go away!" Sion wanted to shout his response, but kept his volume down. He did not want his parents hearing them argue.

"Oooo, you been trying to draw too! You're not very good. I'm much better at drawing than you. It's not even coloured in!" Gwen made a lunge for the papers on the floor. Sion beat her to it and grabbed the sheets before shoulder barging his sister out of the door and sticking his desk chair under the handle. He stumbled over to his shelf of trinkets and curiosities. Whenever he upset his sister, she'd try to bang on the wall from the other side to dislodge his rock collection from the shelf. In their previous (more modern) house, this had been successful on every occasion. Sion doubted if a ten year old girl could hit a solid stone wall hard enough to make a shelf shake. He was correct. There was a small, muffled thump sound, but nothing happened.

"Idiot," Sion mumbled under his breath, as he carefully hid his papers and pens back under the bed.

Chapter 8

Can We Make it Further?

Thankfully, when Saturday morning came, the morning sun came with it. The glow seeped into Sion's room, becoming brighter as the sun rose above the heather-lined hill tops. As soon as he noticed the apparent change in the weather conditions, Sion flew out of his bed, dressed and retrieved his rucksack. He'd prepared a bag for just such a morning. It contained a bottle of water, one of his dad's torches, a hat, dog poo bags, fold up waterproof coat, pens, paper, a packet of raisins and a square of Kendal Mint Cake. His parents always seemed to have some when they went walking, so it must be a good idea. Sion scribbled two brief notes for his mum, one for upstairs and one for downstairs, to let her know that he'd taken Albert for a walk and would be back by 9am. This would be ample time to get back to the cave for another look.

Doesn't it always seem to be that when you're trying to be quiet, it's as if someone has turned the volume up on the house? Every step, every door, every floor board makes more noise than it ever has before. At least Albert didn't make too much fuss when Sion beckoned him with a lead. He seemed to be keener on the idea of a lie in, but with a little persuasion, he ambled over. Sion put his second note next to the kettle, they were bound to go there first. Albert was now eager to go out and he pulled at Sion's arm and began to whine.

"Shhhh! Don't you dare wake them all up, you muppet!" Sion whispered. He carefully unlocked and opened the back door, slipped out with Albert and cautiously pulled it to, again. It was then that Sion remembered the gravel. Why did it have to be gravel? He stood still on the doorstep and tried to visualise a way around to the gate without stepping on the stones. He knew they'd alert one of his family with their crunching underfoot. Albert was getting restless. Sion motioned Albert to walk next to him, along the flower bed, onto the manhole cover and across to the road. Paws did tread in the gravel once or twice, but barely made a sound.

Sion was prepared for Albert to jump the kissing gate, this time. Once again, he cleared it with ease before waiting patiently for Sion to come the conventional way. The two of them almost ran the length of the footpath this time, they seemed to arrive at the foot of the hill in no time at all. Sion paused to see if there was a simpler way up for Albert, who'd struggled with the loose stones on their last visit. How had he missed it? There was a path, a trodden path, not two metres away. Disguised slightly by gorse bushes, it led diagonally up the hill and ended not too far from the cave entrance. Albert bounded up the path, pulling Sion like a husky and sled. His pace left Sion quite breathless as they reached the top, but it had definitely been easier going than the scree covered option. As Sion caught his breath, he looked down at his house. He could see no sign of anyone up and about. He began to wander slowly towards the cave, with a slight feeling of apprehension. What if someone was in there? Would he go in or keep walking? Sion decided that if there was, he'd walk past and go straight home.

He didn't need to worry, the cave was as empty as it had been last time. Sion stopped outside to retrieve his hat and extra coat from his rucksack. He also took out his dad's torch, paper and pens and stuffed a piece of the Kendal Mint Cake into his mouth. He blinked repeatedly and shook his head, as the sugar rush hit him. Now he knew why his parents liked it on long walks. Sion closed his bag, put it back onto his back and gestured to Albert to go into the cave. He shone the torch onto the walls. His dad's torch was much better, it lit up the walls more clearly and made spotting the markings for a second time, simple. Sion crept closer to the wall and leaned in to examine the scribbles and scratches. There it was, clear as crystal. The brighter light made it so obvious. Inside a large scratched square was a circle, split into sections, like a cut pie. Half of them were a greenish brown, the other half were redder in tone. Sion had been right. He swallowed and took a step back, as he did, treading on a paw. The yelp from Albert echoed in the cave like a pack of howling wolves. Sion panicked and darted out of the cave. He checked Albert's paw and apologised to him, hoping that animals could understand when you were genuinely sorry. Composing himself, Sion took his water from his bag, drank half of it and offered the rest to Albert. He seemed very grateful and lapped haphazardly at the trickle as Sion slowly tipped the bottle. He checked his watch, it was nearly half past eight. "We'd best get back, lad," Sion sighed. He put his rucksack back on and started off towards the diagonal track on the hillside.

As they came in through the back door, Sion's mum was reading his note by the kettle. She looked up and smiled.

"Nice walk? Did Albert do any business?"

"Yes thanks," Sion replied cheerfully. "And no, he didn't poo."

His mother winced slightly, it was her dislike of saying 'poo' out loud.

"OK, love. No problem. Would you like a tea?"

"Please," replied Sion. "A big one!"

Chapter 9

But Who?

The notes and scribbles under Sion's bed were becoming more and more detailed by the day. He had annotated sketches of the markings, drawings and notes about the footpaths and a list of possibilities about the cave itself. How far did it go? How frequently was the fire used and whom by? Each day, he would make sure he'd done something, anything to add to his growing project. It fascinated him. The mystery of the symbols, the location of the cave and how deep it went into the hill, the possible, no definite link to Tarquin. Sion wanted to know more about Tarquin. Who is he? Where does he live? Why does he have the symbol from the cave on his neck? He recalled that Tarquin's tattoo was small, it hadn't been obvious, couldn't have been bigger than a two pence coin. But it was definitely the same style as the one on the damp cave wall. Question after question popped into Sion's head, occasionally he said them out loud to himself, it helped him to concentrate when he repeated them this way. Not an hour went by in a day, when Sion wasn't thinking about it. Unfortunately, the weather had once again halted his progress. He didn't mind walking in the rain, he enjoyed real weather. It had so often been nothing but a white sky, back in England. At least here there was weather, even if it often meant torrential rain and strong gales. When the sun came out, it was wonderful! The problem was, walking in rain and wind is one thing, but tackling a scree covered slope and a narrow hilltop path in such conditions was getting on to life threatening, at times.

During his breakfast on Monday, Sion hatched a plan. He munched noisily on his toast, while staring ahead. Due to his mother's gluten intolerance, Sion, his father and sister were also expected to eat the 'free from' bread. Sion didn't like it. Toasted, it was just about bearable, but if they needed sandwiches, it was, in his opinion, inedible. To make his breakfast more palatable, Sion had slathered his doorstop sized slice in lashings of butter and Marmite. He was the only one in his family who ate it, which pleased him, as there was always the same amount in the jar as he'd left.

As he devoured the final mouthful of toast, Sion scanned the room for something. He was looking for a piece of paper. It was smaller than A5 and had a logo with a lorry, at the top. That piece of paper was the receipt for the removal company. He'd seen it a few times floating about the house and last time, he was sure it had been in the kitchen. Surely, this paper had a number or an email, a way for Sion to contact Tarquin. He so desperately wanted to speak to him.

Sion casually walked around the kitchen while he finished his orange juice, scanning every surface for the paper. He could imagine it everywhere. As he put his empty glass on the side and turned to go, he caught sight of it, sticking out from behind a phone bill on the cork board, was a lorry logo. He was just about to reach for it when he stopped. His mother and sister, who were still at the table, would think it odd that Sion wanted a receipt for the removals company. He was going to have to come back later, when he wouldn't be seen. Maybe he could just copy the contact details onto his notes, so as not to disturb the paperwork. Clearly it had been put there so it was safe.

Dressing slowly, Sion looked up at the cave from his window. It seemed so far away today, always did on misty days.

Every few minutes, it'd disappear behind a shroud of mist, then reappear as the curtain moved on. Each time, adding to its mystery. Pulling his shoes on, Sion sat on the ledge seat under the large window. As he glanced up again, he froze, the laces of his trainers dropped down from his fingers. He frantically ferreted for his binoculars. A figure had emerged from the cave. It had definitely come from inside, he was certain of that. Through the binoculars, Sion could make out that it was a man, not large. He was wearing a hat and appeared to be eating something warm, as Sion could see steam rising from whatever was in his hand. Maybe a fire had been lit again. Sion continued to watch the man through the binoculars. After finishing the steaming food, he sat on the rock by the cave, the same rock as Sion had used. A few minutes later, the man returned to the cave, before coming back to the path, this time carrying a bag. He then began to walk along the track, around the hill, before disappearing out of view. Sion lowered the binoculars and looked up at the hill and to the point where the man had vanished. His eyes were straining and began to water. He needed Tarquin and he needed him now!

While his parents and Gwen had been cleaning the car, Sion had speedily scribbled the number and email from the top corner of the paper, onto the inside cover of his notebook. He made sure not to write who it was, so that if his sister got hold of his belongings again, she'd have no idea who the details belonged to.

Even being a confident boy in most situations, Sion wasn't happy with the idea of ringing the removal company. So with several other tabs open, to click on quickly, he began to write an email. He kept it simple and pretended to be his father, just wanting to ask a question about an item in the lorry, requesting correspondence with Tarquin, personally.

Send. It had gone, now he must wait.

For the rest of the morning, Sion paced about, not really settling on any activity or conversation. Not helping his mood, was the prospect of starting his new school in a week's time. His mother had mentioned something at breakfast about buying new uniforms later today. How on earth was he going to concentrate on that nonsense? As the thought rushed around his head, his mum called upstairs.

"You ready, Sion? It's time to go into town. Make sure you brush your teeth, you've had Marmite!"

"Alright!" Sion responded, trying to sound more enthusiastic than he was.

He'd gathered that his uniform had an actual tie. He'd never had a tie before and had no idea how to do one.

To his relief, when they arrived in town, the assistant in the shop informed them of a change to the school's uniform. Apparently they had recently become an academy and had changed their tie, shirt and blazer to a polo shirt and round-neck jumper combo. Much more sensible, in Sion's opinion. So, two pairs of grey trousers, three white polo shirts and two purple jumpers were purchased for Sion. Gwen was less impressed by her blue dress and grey checked cravat. She huffed and puffed and whined when asked to try things on. Their mother reminding her several times that she'd only got one year left in the junior school, before she'd need a uniform like Sion's. This coupled with the promise of junk food for their late lunch, improved Gwen's mood a little.

It was while staring at a burger box that Sion remembered how his day had begun. This month's kids' meal promotion was for an animated film, which included cave dwelling characters. Sion stared at the cave in the picture. He visualised the man from this morning sitting outside. He'd definitely been eating something, something hot. If he'd used the campfire, it'd be obvious, especially if food had been cooked there. Maybe there'd be some rubbish left. Or would he be too smart to do that? Sion tried to work out when he'd be able to go up there again. Today was a write off, surely. It was past 2pm now. They were calling at the supermarket on the way home, so they'd not be back until at least four o'clock and then it'd be nearly time to eat again. Was he brave enough to sneak out at night? He shuddered at the thought. No, he wasn't ready for that, not even with Albert as company.

"Sion, Sion! Have you listened to anything I've said?" Sion's mother sounded irritated.

"Er," Sion began, "No, sorry, I was miles away."

"I said, what do you fancy for dinner tonight? Gwen wants Bolognese. That ok with you?" She looked at him and gestured towards his sister, who was nodding frantically at him.

"Yeah," Sion agreed. "Bolognese is fine with me. Can we have garlic bread too?"

"No problem. I'll get you and Gwen a proper one. That gluten free one was really chewy, wasn't it?" Sion's mum said, looking at him and Gwen in turn.

"Yeah, it was revolting! Wasn't it, Gwen?"

Gwen grunted and nodded as she continued to chomp her way through her fries, slathering each one in gelatinous barbecue sauce.

The supermarket stop didn't last as long as Sion had dreaded. They were turning onto the gravel drive before half past three. Albert was in the window. They couldn't hear him, but he was clearly barking their arrival. Dribble and drool splattering onto the glass at every woof. Sion's mum grumbled something about running out of window cleaner, as she opened the car boot.

"Help me please, you two!" She yelled, as Sion and Gwen went to woof back at Albert from the outside of the window.

Between the three of them, the bags were heaved into the kitchen and everything put away. Sion's mum was preparing to chop an onion as he sneaked quietly upstairs to check his emails. He was pleased that on his last birthday, his father had removed the security setting from his account which forwarded all emails to his parents' account. It hadn't seemed a big deal at the time, but today, it was a godsend.

Two new emails. Sion rarely got one, so two was a good sign. He opened the first one, it was from the office at the removal company. They'd forwarded his email to Tarquin. Good start, Sion thought. Email two.

"Yes!" Sion shouted out loud. It was from Tarquin! Well he presumed it was, the email address had 'quinny' in it. Sion quivered with a mixture of excitement, anticipation and angst. Click.

Hi Mr Roberts,

I hope you've settled in well. There was nothing else in the van when we got back to the depot, I'm afraid. What is it you're missing?

I'll look out for a reply and will help in any way I can.

Tarquin

Now was Sion's chance to own up. He began to type a reply.

Hi Tarquin,

It's not Mr Roberts actually, it's me, Sion. I really need to speak to you about something.

I've found a cave and there's a symbol there, like your tattoo. You said you knew the area. I just wondered how you knew it and if you know about the symbol on the cave wall. Also someone is using the cave for a fire, I saw him this morning. I don't know what else to say or ask really. Just thought you could help me.

Hope to hear from you soon.

Sion.

Click. Sion had never wanted to get a reply to anything, more than he wanted a reply from Tarquin. But, he knew that it wasn't going to come straight away, so closing his laptop, Sion slipped back downstairs. The smell of frying mince and onions hit him four steps from the bottom. The delicious aroma made his stomach groan with hunger. Junk food never satisfied his appetite for long. The kitchen was steamy from the large pan of water on the hob. Sion pulled a face when he saw the gluten free spaghetti. It always clumped together in a mass of undercooked mess. He stirred the Bolognese with the ancient wooden spoon, his mother loved her traditional kitchenalia; she couldn't resist a look in charity shops for random bits and bobs. His mum appeared next to him and tipped the spaghetti into the boiling water. The water erupted to the brim of the pan, before calming down.

"Stir the pasta for me, Sion," his mother requested. "It'll clump if it's left."

Sion stirred the opaque water and attempted to bash the spaghetti apart on the side of the pan.

He quite enjoyed helping in the kitchen, maybe because his mother was calmer when she was cooking. She knew recipes by heart, just used books for inspiration, not for exact instruction. She knew measurements by eye or by feel. It was the one time that she was spontaneous.

After ten more minutes, dinner was served. Sion had forgotten about the expectant email. He was too busy serving up spaghetti onto four warmed plates. Albert waited patiently by his side for any spillage, looking from Sion's face to the pan and back, while unsuccessfully licking drool from his lips, which frequently splattered onto the quarry tiles below. Sion was pleased with his pasta cooking work, he was yet to find a clump of hard spaghetti. The family took their seats at the large kitchen table and tucked into their steaming plates, as the gluten packed garlic bread was passed between Sion and Gwen.

Chapter 10

Something is Better than Nothing, Right?

The next morning came. Still no reply.

By seven o'clock on Friday evening, Sion had lost all hope of Tarquin responding at all. He was angry that in his last week of holiday, he'd felt like he'd wasted his time. He would be at school next week and back to the crazy term time routines.

Why? Why had Tarquin ignored him? Of course it was possible that he'd not seen the email yet, but it was unlikely. Maybe Tarquin was angry with Sion for contacting him or that he'd pretended to be his father. Whatever the reasons, Sion was miserable and had been unpleasant to be around. He'd even been annoying himself.

Then, at half past eight on Saturday evening, his laptop made a sound, a barely audible 'ping'. Sion reacted like a bird of prey, swooping across his room and snatching the laptop from the desk.

Hi Sion,

Sorry for taking a while to reply to you. I'll be honest, your email took me by surprise. I knew you'd find it. It was only a matter of time. I can tell you know little at the moment, but I'm very impressed that you remembered my tattoo, you must have only seen it for a second or two. I'm not going to explain much in an email. All I'll say is, my tattoo and the cave marking are the same, I do know the area and I think I know who you saw. I presume you'll be back at school soon. I hope you enjoy it. Please don't discuss this with any new friends, yet. All will become clearer, I promise. I'll be in touch soon.

Good luck with school.

Quinny.

Even though he knew little more now than he did five minutes ago, Sion was happy. Happy in the knowledge that he'd know more soon and that things were definitely going to get more exciting from now on.

Chapter 11

Tarquin

Tarquin Edward Williams doesn't share his personal details, unless it's absolutely necessary. And that's just how he likes it, thank you very much. Over the years, the snippets of information, which have been divulged, for one reason or another, have been few and far between. They have, however, been enlightening, to say the least.

As a larger than average school boy, growing up in Wales with the initials TEW, was problematic at times. He regularly cursed his mother's limited Welsh language skills, whenever he was being reminded of his naming irony by 'comedians' at break times. To add to that, Tarquin had to contend with the constant jibes about his parents' employment. Before he came along (rather unexpectedly) Tarquin's mother had been a trapeze artist for an international circus troupe. He was never 100% sure, but he was led to believe that his father had been a weightlifter with the same troupe. Tarquin had met this gentleman on the odd occasion, when he was still in primary school, but after the age of about nine or ten, any correspondence had dried up and he had not seen him since. At around the same time, Tarquin gained a half-sister. A petite girl with blonde curls, so long she could sit on them. They muddled along as siblings through childhood, but Antoinette and Tarquin's ties were cut after an incident in their twenties. Whatever was said that day, ensured that neither brother nor sister would even attempt contact with each other again.

Sometimes, Antoinette would pop into Tarquin's thoughts, and maybe he into hers, but he'd become accomplished at bringing the fog down on these thoughts, as quickly as they'd appeared.

Now, as a self-confessed semi-vagabond, Tarquin spends most of his time enjoying his own company in his van. After a failed attempt to get onto the housing market in his early thirties, he made the decision to live and work in one vehicle. He does own a small tent, just in case he fancies a change or a bit of wild camping on the hills, but nine times out of ten, the van is his home and that's also, just how he likes it!

Tarquin works freelance for a variety of removal companies. He's the reliable option, when they need a strong pair of arms and a bit of extra space. Choosing his hours and his jobs is just perfect and in line with his nomadic living style. And this is just what happened when he got the call to help Sion's family. An extra bit of moving space and an extra pair of hands, with a side helping of Welsh, country lane knowledge.

Once acquainted with the Cave Dwellers (you'll need to read on for that), Tarquin chose to display his loyalty in the best way he could think of; a tattoo. A permanent pledge of his devotion to his underground friends.

Chapter 12

Third Time Lucky?

The alarm clock did not surprise Sion. He'd been lying awake most of the night, his eyes constructing shapes and movements on the ceiling. He currently knew nobody at his school, well he'd met one teacher when he went for a look around over a month ago, but he couldn't remember the man's face, just that he had trousers that were too short and brightly coloured socks. Sion slowly slipped out of his bed, feeling around the floor for his slippers with his cold foot. His mother had put his clean uniform ready on his chair, even his shiny new shoes were tucked underneath, with new black socks stuffed inside. Sion dressed quickly and sat on his window seat, looking up at the cave. It was a clear day, perfect for a walk. He was so disappointed that instead of more adventure, he was having to go to school. As he stared at the opening in the hillside and the footpath, he began to daydream about his next walk. He really wanted to know how deep the cave went, he'd intended to find out last time, but after Albert's echoing yelp had terrified him, he hadn't been keen to go back in. Next time, he would make that his priority. He'd be miffed now if the cave only went another few metres inside after the markings. The dripping certainly sounded like it came from farther away, or that could just have been the echo. Sion was completely engrossed in thought when his mother appeared through the door, her presence startled him.

"Do you want me to make you some porridge, Sion?" she asked gently. She'd clearly anticipated his low mood.

"Yes please," Sion replied. "Can I have a bit of chocolate spread in it?"

"Certainly, just today though. We're not getting into a habit of chocolate breakfasts!" Sion's mother wagged her finger towards him, but only in jest. She meant it though. She was not a fan of sugar packed cereals, especially the chocolate variety.

Sion followed his mother downstairs. As he passed her door, Sion could see that Gwen was still asleep. Her school was not starting back until tomorrow. He grunted a disgruntled grunt and continued down to the kitchen, where his mother was making proper porridge in a saucepan. It made it so creamy and delicious. Sion knew this was a first day back treat and he was going to devour every mouthful. And he did. It was scrumptious! He had changed his mind about the chocolate spread though and opted for a big blob of golden syrup instead and a handful of raisins. Sion didn't eat a lot of sweet things, but he loved syrup. If he had his own way, he would consume a whole tin, spoon by spoon. He was fairly sure though, that his teeth would pay the price, if he did do that.

The time seemed to fly by between eating porridge and needing to leave. Sion checked his bag and stuffed his lunchbox in, noting that his mum had bought his favourite crisps. She was obviously trying to comfort him as much as she could. Before leaving the house, Sion was greeted in the kitchen by Gwen and his father. Totally out of character, Gwen gave Sion a huge hug, squeezing him so tightly he was sure one foot came off the floor. His father was more casual. A few pats on the back and a brief word of encouragement. As he got into the car, Sion looked up again at the cave. He stopped and stared. There were two people standing outside it. One seemed to be large in size and in the same clothing, long black coats and some form of hat, also dark in colour. The engine started. One last look. Both figures disappeared. Disappeared inside the cave. Sion knew at that moment that no matter how fantastic his school was, his mind would definitely be on other matters all day! The cave adventure took another curious turn.

The day didn't drag as much as Sion had worried it would. He made a few new friends, whose company he had genuinely enjoyed and he'd met four teachers. Three of whom were great. One was annoying and it was clear from the reactions and comments from other class members that she was not a popular teacher. She was an older lady, probably close to retirement age and looked as if she'd had a tiring life, smoked for decades or both. Most of Sion's classes had been fun, with lots of laughs, smiles and chatter. As the class walked into Mrs Anderson's room, they made few sounds. They sat at desks and all seemed to want to be as far away from the front as possible. Sion had sat on a desk three rows from the back, next to a boy called Morgan, whom he'd met at break time. Morgan had been kind to Sion and had invited him to join his friends. He was a keen footballer and could talk endlessly about his beloved Everton. During their time in Mrs Anderson's class, they'd been told about the topics they'd be covering during the school year. Mrs Anderson was the school's RE teacher and was a cliché RE teacher. In Sion's previous school, he'd loved RE, as the teacher had been young and enthusiastic. He'd made the world's religions so interesting, really brought them to life. Sion was confident, after just one hour with Mrs Anderson, that she was the polar opposite as far as teachers go. She muttered, sat for the duration and read from a sheet. She looked up occasionally, mainly to scold someone for making a sound. A part of her spiel included a list of things she didn't like, they included; Velcro noise; chewing gum; finger clicking; chairs being dragged instead of lifted; the smell of salt and vinegar crisps and fountain pens. Surely she must have been at the school for decades, as Sion couldn't imagine her successfully completing an interview with such a lack of charisma.

So apart from meeting Mrs Anderson, Sion's day had been a positive one. Despite this, he was desperate to get home and check his emails. He wanted to let Tarquin know that he'd seen people at the cave. Maybe he'd already know, maybe he was one of them. One was large, after all. Once home, Sion ran inside shouting something about needing a wee and headed for his room. He opened the laptop and clicked the email tab. Sion silently fist pumped the air when he saw the new message.

Hi Sion,

Hope your day went well. Saw you leaving. Did you see me? I didn't wave, I've not let them know you know, if that makes sense. I met up with someone to discuss a few things. I've explained a few things for you in a notebook. If you go into the cave, there's a trio of stones on your left. Have a look behind the largest. I just want to say, there's nothing for you to worry or be nervous about, but plenty to be curious about.

All will become clear, over time.

I'm sure one day soon, we'll chat again in person.

Let me know when you've been and that you've found the information. Hopefully you'll be able to go soon, even if you are back at school.

Regards

Tarquin

"Wow!" Sion remarked quietly, as he leant back on his desk chair. He needed to get up there very quickly and find this information. Maybe he'd put it into a small bag or box.

It was then that Sion remembered that he was supposed to be going to the toilet. He closed the laptop and scooted back downstairs, dashing into the bathroom to flush the toilet.

Sion's mother announced that their dinner was going to be later than planned as his father had been delayed by roadworks on the dual carriageway. Perfect.

"Mum, can I take Albert for a quick walk?"

"Yes," she replied. "That'd be great, he's only been in the garden today. I'm sure he'd love to stretch his legs. But please get changed first, I don't have time to wash a set of uniform tonight."

Sion needed no more encouragement, he was off up the stairs and changed within minutes. Grabbing his rucksack and coat, he made his way downstairs, jumping the final five steps and shouting Albert's name. Not fifteen minutes later, Sion and Albert were outside the cave, both puffing and panting. They'd made it up in record time. Torch on, they padded carefully inside. Sion glanced briefly at the markings again and at the campfire, which had obviously been used recently, the soot and charred wood were different to before. Sion stepped further inside and scanned around the left side for three stones. They were several metres farther in than the markings. Sion felt anxious, which annoyed him. He so wanted to feel brave. The dripping sound was louder here, it sounded like drips falling into deep water, not just a puddle on the floor. Self-preservation took over and told Sion to not go farther than necessary. He felt behind all of the stones, they all seemed to be of a similar size. Wrapped in a carrier bag, he found a small notebook, tucked well under the stone closest to the wall. He stuffed the book, still wrapped up, into his rucksack and turned to leave. Then he remembered what he'd promised himself. Sion turned back to face the inside of the cave. He shone the torch around. He could see nothing. It seemed to go on forever. The dripping he'd heard told him that there must be a drop somewhere, so any further investigation would require caution. Maybe he should ask Tarquin about that. He wouldn't want Sion to hurt himself, or worse. If it was too dangerous, he'd say.

Albert gestured for Sion to leave. Half way down the diagonal track, Albert stopped.

"Oh for crying out loud!" Sion said irritably as he pulled two small black bags from his rucksack pocket. Typically the rain began to lash down as he bent to clean up after his now relieved dog. The horizontal rain soaked both walkers within seconds, but had stopped by the time they reached the back door. Sion's mum could be heard yelling, as Albert galloped into the kitchen, his muddy paws smearing vast quantities of dirt across the recently mopped tiles. He was quickly manoeuvred into the utility room and a towel put down for him to lie on. Sion removed his wet shoes and coat before scuttling up to his room to examine the book. He paused just inside his door. Maybe it would be better to look later, when he was more confident of not being disturbed. Gwen would be in bed by eight o'clock. The bag, with book inside, was stuffed back under the bed and Sion grabbed a dry jumper, before returning to the kitchen to investigate the dinner situation. His walk had worn him out and he required an energy boost, quickly. He was pleased to see his mother with a pizza in her hand.

"This ok, Sion?" His mum asked wearily. "It's not gluten free. You can share it with Gwen. I'll do beans."

"Yeah!" Sion replied approvingly. "Perfect. I'm starving!"

Chapter 13

Do I Need to Read it All?

Gwen's bedtime did not run as smoothly as usual, due to her anxiety about starting her new school in the morning. Half past eight past and she was still protesting to her mother, whose patience was definitely faltering. Finally, at just gone nine o'clock, all was quiet. Sion, who was sitting in the lounge with his father watching David Attenborough, glanced up as his mother trudged into the room and collapsed onto the sofa wearily.

"Is it time for you to go up now, Sion?" His mother asked with a sigh.

"Yeah, maybe. I think this bison might have had it anyway," he replied as he got up and headed to the door.

Sion plodded up the stairs, brushed his teeth and returned to his room. Retrieving the wrapped notebook from under his bed, he sat on the rug. The bag was still damp, but the notebook was dry, thankfully. Tarquin had written Sion's name onto the front. His handwriting was impeccable. Proper cursive style, like you'd see on an old manuscript.

His hands began to shake slightly as he lifted the cover of the spiral-bound notebook. Sion gasped at the quantity of writing and drawings inside. He skimmed it through quickly, with his thumb, like a child's flick book. He was never going to be able to digest all of this information this evening, he'd got school again in the morning. Sion glanced at his watch. 21:20.

If he allowed himself until ten o'clock, then surely he'd learn something useful. He clambered into bed, under the duvet, but not enough to block the light. Lying on his front, Sion began to read.

Chapter 14

Cave Essentials

Sion, you must always remember that the cave is not a safe place. I doubt you've been too far inside yet, but I can tell you it goes a lot further than you may realise. You collected this notebook from behind the three stones (I'll come onto those later), after the stones, the ground becomes very uneven and there is a drop down. You may have been aware of the water dripping there. It drops approximately 12ft, into a pool. The pool is understandably bitterly cold, no matter what time of year.

Now, if you don't fall down the aforementioned hole, there is a narrow path, maybe only 10 inches in width, running to the right of The Drop. It is usable and there are handles on the wall, they're not all secure, so take care with those. I know it sounds risky, but you get used to it.

If you did fall into the pool, all is not lost. It'll be frightening, as it's dark, but if you swim to your right, you'll find the wall quickly and there are ledges to climb back up. I know this because I did fall in once. Thought I was a goner. Thank goodness for my head torch being waterproof!

Like I mentioned before, the three stones. They're not just three stones, as you may have gathered. They are significant. Extraordinarily significant.

Before anyone crosses The Drop, they must turn the stones. Each stone has part of The Mark, my mark, the mark you saw. It's etched onto the stones, on the edges. These marks must be aligned, to form a triangle. They're magnets, of sorts. They'll move themselves back after a time.

Just to clarify, the journey is around the edge, not into The Drop.

Sion stared at the sketched diagram underneath. It was detailed, especially considering it was of an almost pitch dark place. Tarquin had labelled the diagram and taken time to draw the three stones in both positions. He was clearly an artist. Professional or not. He was a talented man, wasted on house removals.

After one final look at the drawings, Sion closed the notebook. He was mentally exhausted from reading that first section. That and it being his first day at school too. He tucked the notebook back into his rucksack. He'd almost put it under his pillow, but had imagined his mother stripping his bed while he was out and assuming it was rubbish. That would've been a disaster!

After turning off his bedroom light, Sion lay almost motionless on his back, hands under his head, staring up at the ceiling. He'd not closed his curtains and the glow of the gibbous moon filled his room with a beautiful dim light. He visualised himself turning the stones and thought about how heavy they might be. Maybe they're much lighter than they look. Even though Tarquin had said it wasn't a crisis, Sion really did not want to land in the pool at the bottom of The Drop. Why did Tarquin consistently capitalise The Drop? It must be its actual name. He imagined creeping along the ledge, trying to hold onto anything that was secure. Tarquin hadn't actually said how far you had to walk along the ledge. Surely it can't be that far.

Part of Sion wanted to get the notebook back out and carry on, but he knew he'd never sleep. He must take his time and make sure he took in as much as possible. Rushing through such a quantity of information could literally result in death! He wanted adventure, but his head was screwed on too. Right now his mind needed to rest.

Chapter 15

Will I be as Lucky Next Time?

Over his first week at school, Sion had decided not to visit the cave. The weather hadn't been great and most days, after homework and dinner, it was too late or dark for a walk. Also, Sion had realised that if he was going to navigate the ledge above 'The Drop', he wouldn't be able to take Albert with him. This was adding a whole new problem. How would he explain going for, what could be, a very long walk, without the dog? His parents would definitely consider this to be strange and may even tell him that he couldn't go at all. Sion hatched a plan, not a fantastic one, but it'd do for now. He was going to explain to his parents that he'd been watching some interesting birds and that to use his binoculars successfully, he really needed to go out without the dog sometimes. He decided that this would go down better if he did take Albert out at some point, even if just for a few minutes.

So, that was that, on Saturday morning, after scoffing down his cereal, Sion announced his intention, in a planned, blasé fashion.

"No problem, Sion. Glad you're enjoying the wildlife so much," his dad responded. "I'll be taking Albert out later anyway. I'm going to wander down to the pub to meet some guys from work. They're doing a day walk and will be finishing at the, er, Bull."

Sion corrected his father. "Y Tarw, dad."

"Yeah, that," his father replied sheepishly. He wasn't confident to attempt Welsh words, yet.

Sion didn't want to waste any more of his time, he ran upstairs, three steps at a time and retrieved his bag. Checked it for the notebook and the torch. He wouldn't need poo bags, but he'd best get his binoculars. If his father saw them left, there would be questions. As Sion left through the back door, his father was busy sanding an old door, on the step.

"Enjoy! Let me know what you see. We'll have to get you a little book, so you can identify them."

Sion didn't turn to reply, he just lifted his thumb into the air.

His heart was racing. He hadn't even begun the hill. He needed to stop and calm down. He turned to face his house, hands on hips. He began to talk to himself about how Tarquin surely wouldn't be intentionally sending him to certain peril. This was exciting, he needed to get a grip and enjoy the adventure. He continued to walk. On his arrival outside the cave, he removed the notebook from his rucksack and read quickly through the first page again. Then he began to think. Where on earth was he going? He must be mad!

"Come on!" Sion encouraged himself to his feet, turned on the torch, put his rucksack back onto his back and walked in. Shining the torch onto the three stones, he could see that they were how they should be. Relief filled his mind. He bent down and rubbed his hands over the stones. They were smooth, even the painted markings were. He wondered how easy they were going to be to move. It was silent, apart from the continuous dripping of water into The Drop.

Big puff out and Sion reached down to move the stones into position. It was simple, as if they were just sitting on the ground, not attached to anything. As he turned the final stone to create the symbol, a small light appeared in the distance. Water reflected it. It seemed so far away. Or was it just small? Sion got to his feet and shone his torch towards The Drop. It looked terrifyingly deep, but he'd been reassured by Tarquin's explanation. He could clearly see the ledge at the side. With his legs trembling, Sion stepped onto the smooth rock. He felt the wall for the handles that Tarquin had mentioned and quickly found one. Slowly, one apprehensive step after another, Sion made his way along the ledge, holding the torch in his mouth. There was a slight overhang at one point, which required Sion to lean over The Drop more than he'd hoped. All his faith was in the strength of the handles. His rucksack sagged down as his body arched around the overhang. Sion's heart was racing. He let go of the handle in his left hand and frantically felt around for the next. As he touched it, his fingers clasped and he swung his right hand across to the previous handle. He stood motionless for a moment, savouring the lack of overhang. The torch in his mouth was making him gag and dribble. With one hand, he took the torch and shone it around. It seemed that there was only one more handle to go. The little light he'd seen from the other side was closer and appeared to be about ten metres away. Sion stuffed the torch back into his mouth, felt for the final handle and pulled himself across, onto the cave floor ahead. He'd made it. Terrified, but he'd made it. He shone the torch around again. Nothing much to see, he could still hear from dripping water, now behind him. He lit the floor in front of him, it seemed stable. He began to slowly walk towards the light. As he drew closer, Sion could see a door shape on the left wall, the light seemed to be coming from a small hole at the top. He wasn't sure why, as he'd not read that far yet, but it seemed clear that this was the way to go next. Sion slowly pushed at the door. It opened, brightness causing him to blink and filling his eyes with water. As he moved the door further, the light that had guided him, vanished with a sharp snapping noise, like a mouse trap. Maybe the stones were moving back too. Sion jumped, panicking slightly. Despite this, he stepped through the door, his eyes adjusting more by the second, to the glaring light.

Carefully pulling the door to, behind himself, Sion stood still and tried to survey the area. It was a colossal cave, but full of light, which seemed to be all around him. Sion tried to make out where it was coming from. He glanced around and tried to focus on one of the sources, closer to him. His eyes moved towards where he stood.

"Glow worms," he whispered to himself, as he gazed open mouthed. "There must be thousands of them."

"Actually, I think it's millions," came a voice from beside him.

Sion swore. He didn't often, but this was exceptional circumstances. Standing not two metres away, was a person. Male, smaller than Sion, with long straggly grey hair, which was tied back in a band. He wore linen trousers with brown, leather sandals and as Sion's eyes moved up, he noticed that the diminutive gentleman was indeed wearing a black, Metallica t-shirt. Exactly the same one as Sion's father wore when he was decorating.

"Nice shirt," Sion stammered.

The gentleman looked down at the shirt and sniggered. "Yes, a friend brought it for me."

Sion could imagine Tarquin buying a gift like this. With his courage growing, he continued his conversation. "What's your friend's name?"

"Quinny," the gentleman responded with a smile. Clearly, he was fond of him. "I'm Geoff, by the way." A small hand was held out to shake. Sion shook it gently and replied,

"I'm Sion. It's, er, nice to meet you, Geoff."

Hundreds of questions filled Sion's head again, but he was lost for words. Aware of his apprehension, Geoff beckoned Sion to follow him down the steps.

"Do you like tea?" Geoff asked without turning around. "Quinny loves it! Always have to get the water on when he's coming."

"Er, yeah, I do. Thanks." Sion still wasn't quite sure what he was doing, but felt more at ease if Tarquin knew this person. He followed Geoff to another door and was led through to a room, filled to the brim with furniture and ornaments. Geoff showed Sion to a seat, before disappearing through a doorway, hopefully to make tea. Sion sat, scrutinising the room. He'd never seen so many things in one place and the patterns and colours everywhere. It was incredible, like the fashions from several decades, all rolled into one. Sitting open-mouthed, Sion was unaware of Geoff returning with a tray, laden with cups, a teapot, milk jug, sugar bowl and what looked like biscuits.

"Tea's up. How do you like it?" Geoff enthusiastically enquired.

"Er, just milk please," Sion stammered again.

"Biscuit?" asked Geoff, holding the plate up, towards Sion's face. "They're dandelion cookies, I made them yesterday. Delicious, if I do say so myself."

Sion took a biscuit and subtly tried to sniff it. It did actually smell very appetising, with its syrupy scent. Sion waited for Geoff to bite a large chunk from his, before beginning on his own. Geoff was right, they were delicious.

The feeling of caution and fear had left Sion. He felt relaxed, sipping tea with Geoff. Occasionally, he'd remind himself that actually, this was unusual and that he should still be wary of his surroundings and indeed of Geoff. He seemed very friendly and he knew Tarquin, of course, but still, sitting in this multi-coloured, jam-packed room, in a cave, with a man shorter than his younger sister, was by a long shot, the most bonkers thing Sion had ever done.

As he drained the last of his tea, he was suddenly deafened by an ear-splitting alarm sound. Geoff jumped to his feet and ran to the door, opening it with haste and frantically looking around the cave. He rushed back in, took Sion by the hand, giving him just enough time to grab his bag, and pulled him towards the door.

"Go! Go straight up the steps and back out. Get your torch on so you can see the ledge and get home! NOW!" Geoff was clearly panic-stricken, but simultaneously seemed to know what was happening.

"What's going on?" Sion protested as he was thrust up the steps, towards the door.

"Come again, been great to meet you," said Geoff, as if he'd not been asked a question.

"But," Sion stammered, as Geoff pushed him through the door.

"Bye, see you again."

The door was shut with a slam and Sion was plunged into darkness. His eyes were not adjusting at all, he could just make out the entrance to the cave and could hear the familiar dripping sounds. He fiddled about in his bag for the torch. With a click, the cave around him was illuminated. He looked back at the door he'd been unceremoniously shoved through, moments earlier, but it was barely visible. He darted the light around the wall, but nothing. As the light shone across to The Drop, Sion began to wonder if he'd dreamt meeting Geoff. It all seemed too ridiculous to even consider. A man not much more than the height of a metre stick, wearing a Metallica t-shirt, making tea and dandelion biscuits, in a cave lit by glow worms? Sion sighed and shone the torch onto his watch, he'd been out for nearly two hours, he'd best get back. Carefully and slowly he navigated his way back along the ledge, this time tackling the overhang with ease. As he turned to look back over The Drop, he realised that after the door had closed, the sound of the alarm was non-existent. His ears burned with the effort of trying to pick the sound up. It wasn't there. On his way out of the cave, Sion remembered that he was supposed to be spotting birds. As he looked up towards the hills, he saw a buzzard, flying away with a small animal, maybe a rabbit, in its talons.

"That'll do," he said to himself as he slid down the scree and back home.

Chapter 16

Geoff

Geoffrey Orson Davies (Yes, those are his initials!) was born in Gloucestershire, in a small cave network near the Forest of Dean. His father, also a Geoffrey, was uncharacteristically tall, but Geoff had not inherited this height. This was probably a blessing rather than a curse, as being tall was not really befitting of a Cave Dweller. Geoffrey Senior and Mrs Davies still live in the same network and from time to time, Geoff and Katla pay a visit. Unfortunately it's frequently a stressful event, as Geoff's father is insistent that he can't understand Katla's accent and insists on Geoff 'translating' everything she says.

The gate and duties which Geoff so loves, were his father's responsibility, before his retirement. Before taking over from him, Geoff had been a postman of sorts; walking endless miles to move documents and parcels from one network to another. He would be away for days, weeks or even months at a time. It was during this role that Geoff first met Tarquin. To ease the monotony of tramping the networks, Geoff would occasionally walk above ground. It was a break from the gloom and a boost of vitamin D for his pale complexion. While attempting to rejoin a network in the Brecon Beacons, Geoff had dropped his post bag into a deep hole. He was verging on hysterical when Tarquin had happened upon him and had helped to retrieve the bag. Then, only weeks later, Geoff had bumped into Tarquin again. This time they were both a little further north, near Shrewsbury. Geoff had unwittingly surfaced at Hawkstone

Park Follies, a busy tourist attraction with a popular cave walk. On entering the bright light of day, he'd immediately come face to face with Tarquin again, who had been delivering some furniture to the site restaurant. Due to their shared (but very different) obscurity, they had recognised each other in an instant. Geoff asked Tarquin where he was and explained that he'd surfaced in the wrong place, but of course, this led to questions, which eventually Geoff decided to answer. He'd always been a bit of a rebel, albeit a sensible one. He decided there and then that an ally from above ground might be a useful commodity, especially one with a bit of bulk and a kind heart. Geoff had given Tarquin details of how to find him and the rest is history.

It wasn't long after this that Geoff met Katla. He'd been given a tough assignment to deliver a parcel of live glow worm eggs to a network in Ireland. Not only did this entail weeks of walking, but also a ferry crossing. The bag was lumpy and difficult to carry comfortably; glass jars of varying sizes dug into his back and clinked together continuously. That and the abuse he'd been given by a group of men on the ferry, who taunted his size and followed him about, spilling their drinks and generally being unpleasant to all around them. Had it not been for meeting Katla, the whole trip would've been the worst event in his lifetime. But there she was, greeting him just outside the port. He'd been told he'd be met, but had he known it was going to be by a beautiful lady, he'd have made more of an effort to look (and smell) better. Anyway, it mattered not, she obviously liked his unkempt nature and they were smitten before they reached their cave destination.

Chapter 17

How Can No One Know?

After visiting the cave of glow worms, meeting Geoff and hearing the deafening alarm, Tarquin *had* to be contacted again. As he opened up his laptop, Sion noticed that Tarquin had beaten him to it. An email was waiting for him.

Hi Sion,

I gather you met Geoff today. He said you may be feeling a little nervous about going back to see him, as their alarm sounded while you were there. I should've mentioned that earlier on in my notes, sorry. I presume you've only read some of them, as you obviously didn't know that Geoff might meet you at the door.

Anyway, well done for getting there so quickly and don't be nervous about going again. Just read on in your notes. I know this must all be very confusing at the moment, but you'll learn a bit more every day.

Regards,

Quinny

Sion was cross with himself for not reading more of his note book before meeting Geoff. He knew that there was no point in returning without some study time first, so he took the notebook from his bag and thumbed through to the next section.

Along with more intricate drawings and diagrams, Tarquin explained a little more about Geoff, his wife, the light in the door, how the stones actually work and the alarm. Sion was mentally exhausted. He kept rereading that last part about the alarm as he couldn't quite believe it. It seemed ludicrous. How did no one know already, well apart from Tarquin and maybe a few others? He read it again, his eyes were bloodshot from concentrating so hard. He slapped the notebook shut, stuffed it back into his bag and got himself ready for bed. He thought he'd be awake for hours, thinking, but Sion was asleep within minutes.

Just after 5am, Sion was woken suddenly by a loud clap of thunder. Torrential rain was smashing against his bedroom window so hard, as if someone was throwing fistfuls of gravel against it. Another massive lightning strike. There was no chance to count elephants in between the flashes and bangs, they were happening simultaneously, the storm was on top of them. Another. Sion was sitting upright in his bed, hugging his knees. He didn't much care for thunder and lightning. A flash. This time two elephants before the bang. Flash. Five elephants. Sion got up and went to look out of the window. Flash. Seven elephants. Relief. He looked up towards the cave, expecting to see nothing through the darkness, but to his surprise, there was a glowing light. The fire. Someone was using the fire. Sion was thankful that he was inside for the storm, not hanging about alone in a gloomy cave. Although, he was very curious to know who this was. Maybe it was Tarquin or the shorter man he'd seen in the summer. Suddenly the glow from the fire vanished, maybe it'd been extinguished swiftly with water. The morning sun was just beginning to glow, behind the hilltops. The storm had moved on, just drips from the roof into the puddles below could be heard. Sion clambered back into bed and pulled his covers up to his chin. He lay still, staring at the ceiling again, thinking about what he'd read last night. He still couldn't quite believe it. The information that Tarquin had shared was so incredible that Sion was beginning to think that it was a film script, not an actual fact sheet. He just couldn't believe that something so implausible could be real and more to the point, how *he* could know about it when more than 99.9% of the population didn't. Sion and his family had managed to move to a house that faced one of only a handful of entrances to a giant cave network. A network that not only ran under their local area, or even the whole country, but spread far and wide, even reaching Brittany in Northern France and the edge of the Icelandic coast. Tarquin's notes had explained that Geoff was one of thousands, who spent most of their time navigating and protecting the caves. Generally friendly and hospitable people, but certainly not folk to mess with. They're experts in their own martial art style, which uses not only physical skill, but allegedly a psychic ability too. A method of controlling the actions and thoughts of others. Despite being very useful at times, it's not something they do unless absolutely necessary, so Sion was hopeful that Geoff had not used it on him.

Geoff's age had come as a shock to Sion. He was clearly a well weathered man, but Sion hadn't expected him to be pushing two hundred years. If his souvenir ruler from a National Trust shop served him well, he thought that may have been about the time of King George III, but he couldn't be sure without checking. Clearly these cave dwelling people had 'a good innings', as Sion's dad would say. He started making guesses as to how old the oldest cave dweller might be now. He plumped for four hundred, although he wouldn't be surprised if it was a much higher number.

Tarquin had told Sion what the cave dwellers were known as, but had written in red pen that Sion must not use the term in front of them, as they found it offensive. They were known as 'Poblpitw', a Welsh derived name, referring to pitiful or insignificant. Sion could understand why they weren't keen, it was a bit derogatory.

While reading the notebook, there had been one part in particular that had made Sion audibly gasp. The cave dwellers' purpose was to preserve and protect a collection that was housed across the vast cave network. Since their first known existence, they had hoarded treasures and artefacts from every walk of life that they'd encountered. Gems to ceramics, gold to important bones. If they found it, they kept it and had no intention of giving anything up. To keep the caves and contents in perfect condition, the network has vents, every few miles. Only small in size, but just enough to allow air to circulate in the cave system. Apparently the closest one to Sion's house, apart from the entrance, was located in a woodland, not far from Sion's school. As Tarquin explained, despite being essential, the vents can cause a problem, they can be unintentionally stumbled upon by people or animals. This, as Tarquin went on, is the reason for the alarm. If a vent is breached, the closest alarm sounds to alert the cave dwellers, who can then secure the vent with a temporary bung. This can then be removed after an appropriate time, to re-open the vent.

Sion was certain that he'd find out more and more as time went on, but his head was, once again, so full of questions. He wanted to know if they were still collecting new things, whether there had ever been a cave disaster, how he could be their friend and help them, like Tarquin obviously did. Sion also wondered if anyone else *did* know anything about all this. Maybe there was someone or some people who were trying to get into the caves. Maybe that's why they need people like Tarquin to help them.

Chapter 18

Who's Rhodri?

Before heading off to school on Monday morning, Sion had emailed Tarquin back. He asked him a few of his questions and also made clear his intentions to go back as soon as he could. Sion really wanted to know if Tarquin and any other 'helpers' had a name that they were collectively known as. He also wanted to know if Tarquin knew why the cave network started in Wales. Of all the areas, why there? He wasn't sure that he'd get an answer for that, but it was something he definitely wanted to find out.

Now he had actual friends there, Sion was quite looking forward to school. He enjoyed talking to people his own age, playing football at break time and actually, he thoroughly enjoyed some of his lessons. There were plenty of inspiring teachers at Sion's new school whom he genuinely respected and enjoyed. Well, apart from Mrs Anderson. But no one seemed to enjoy her company and the feeling appeared to be mutual.

To Sion's (and most pupils') delight, Mrs Anderson was not at school all day. Despite the impending doom of her returning the following day, Sion and his classmates lapped up the 'free' lesson time. The cover supervisor had no work for them, so the whole class spent the session playing hangman on the interactive whiteboard. Sion twice won a round of applause for vexing the others with 'humanitarianism' and 'posthumously'. The latter, he'd only heard that morning, on the radio, referring to a deceased, 80s popstar, who'd reached number one in the charts.

As the school friends left and waved their goodbyes, at the end of the day, Sion was confident that the next RE lesson would not be as fun. His mother was waiting in her usual spot down the road. As he slid into the car, he thought about his morning email to Tarquin and started thinking positive thoughts about there being a reply waiting for him.

"Good day?" Sion's mother enquired, as the car door shut.

"Yes ma. Especially this morning. I was the champion of hangman!" Sion replied enthusiastically.

His mother looked a little baffled. "Why were you not doing actual school work?"

Sion realised that it had probably sounded a little odd. "Oh. Mrs Anderson, the RE teacher wasn't in and there'd been no work left. It was fun. She's back tomorrow apparently."

As they turned back onto the main road, Sion could see a woodland area behind the last of the school buildings. It seemed like an old woodland as the majority of the trees looked like oak or sycamore, not pine. Sion presumed that this was the woods where the closest vent was. You could obviously walk there with no problem, as there was a footpath sign pointing towards it from the pavement. One lunch time, Sion was going to have a little look around, see if he could find the vent. He doubted he would find it though. He wasn't even sure how big they were, they must be fairly small or everyone would find them. He began to wonder if the vents were subtly marked in any way and if so, how.

Before he knew it, the car was crunching onto the gravel driveway. Gwen was already home with Sion's father, who'd had the day off to do some work on the house. Sion sniggered as he saw his father, through the window, frantically returning a James Bond DVD to its box. Obviously he'd been *really* busy then. After giving Albert a quick head scratch and without much of a word to anyone else, Sion rushed to his room, opened the laptop and checked for a reply. He wasn't disappointed.

Hi Sion,

It'd be great if you visited Geoff again, hopefully next time you'll get more time to chat and will not be disturbed by the alarm. Geoff informs me that the breached vent was a very close one, in a woodland area. They're not 100% sure yet what happened, but it seemed like someone was digging there. All sorted now though, we think.

In answer to your questions, Geoff and the others don't call us anything special, apart from our names and the reason the main cave is in your area is entirely down to when they started using a cave system. Around the time of Rhodri the Great, about 1100 years ago, Geoff's ancestors were finding it increasingly difficult to hide their finds and treasures. The cave was already here, not as big, clearly, but it was here. They decided to create a home inside and it expanded over the years from there. The other two openings eventually joined and now they all work together across the network. Think that just about covers that.

Anyway, must be off. Do let me know when you're next planning a visit. I'll let Geoff know and I might even try to join you.

Regards,

Quinny

Once again, Sion was utterly speechless. This was big, really big, gargantuan in fact. He'd never even heard of Rhodri the Great, but he was sure he must have been important. Sion wondered if they owned anything that belonged to this man, like a sword or a piece of his skeleton. He was so excited, fit to burst, but there was no way he could go back until the weekend and even that was not a certainty. Maybe he was going to have to start going at a different time, like the crack of dawn or even in the night. He wasn't keen on that last idea, the cave was dark enough as it is. He was going to have to think about this one, long and hard, and hatch a plan as soon as possible.

Chapter 19

Accept the Challenge?

To ensure that he could return to the cave whenever necessary, Sion had devised a plan. A plan that he was very proud of. He had explained to his parents that he and some friends had set themselves an exercise challenge, which required them to walk over fifty thousand steps a week and that he'd got a route that he was going to use, most days, to accomplish this. He continued by explaining that he couldn't possibly take Albert every time, as he intended to use a path that had two stiles, which Albert was not very good at. Clearing metre high kissing gates he could do, but climbing up the steps of a stile was too much. There had been one occasion, when Sion had attempted to get Albert over a stile. Despite his dog's distress at the time, Sion hadn't been able to resist taking a photo of the poor hound, straddled across the top, two legs over one side and two over the other. It still made him giggle thinking about it. Since that event, Albert had refused point blank to even begin the steps and when a giant dog refuses, there's not much chance of changing their mind.

Sion's parents seemed to approve of his exercise plan. He'd even created a chart on his laptop to track his progress, which he intended to complete, even if he sometimes had to bend the truth a little; his parents were clearly keen to see his progress. Guilt about lying didn't enter Sion's mind, as he wasn't really lying. He was going to be walking a lot every week and he would be recording his walks on a chart and he would definitely be getting fitter if he was walking up to the cave and back frequently.

Two days before his planned return to the cave, Sion emailed Tarquin. He kept it brief, just explaining when he was planning to go and what he'd told his parents. Tarquin's reply came only an hour later, confirming that he should be there already that day and that he'd let Geoff know. He'd also mentioned something at the end of the message about the overhang above The Drop, but in his excitement and haste to pack up his rucksack, Sion had only glanced over this part.

The morning of his return came around quickly. Sion had already been for a few walks after school, so that he could show his parents his chart and progress. It was 7am on a chilly Saturday morning. There was a glistening frost on the grass as the sun rose from above the hills. The sky was clear, the air was crisp, birdsong and water played their morning tunes. Sion could see his breath in front of him, as he stepped outside onto the gravel. He was glad that he wasn't having to sneak out today, his parents knew that he'd be walking early, as he'd mentioned it the night before. To make sure that he had ample time, he'd said that he'd be home before lunch time. Already noticeably fitter, Sion made it to the cave opening in no time at all, puffing slightly as the cold air raced into his lungs, he needed a few moments to compose himself. Coat zipped firmly to the top, hat on, torch ready, rucksack on both shoulders. Sion went straight to the stones, shone the torch onto them and aligned the symbol. Instantly, the dim light in the distance appeared. Sion carefully made his way to the edge of The Drop. He'd found a way to secure his torch onto his sleeve, using one of Gwen's hair bobbles. It should make it much easier. The first few steps were fine, then came the overhang. Sion remembered what he needed to do and reached across, moving his foot towards the edge.

As his fingers slipped, volts of panic shot through him. Frantically his fingers were grabbing for anything within reach, his feet slipping further and further. Sion thrust himself as powerfully as he could muster towards the light. He knew the ledge wasn't far, maybe just maybe he'd be able to grab onto it. As he reached out, his fingers gripped desperately to the slate, his face also found the ledge. Relief of the apparent act of self-preservation was interspersed with pain. Sion's forehead and nose were throbbing and he could feel the warm trickle of blood running down his face and onto his lips. He stuck his tongue out and spat as he hauled himself onto the ledge, pausing on all fours for a few moments to take in what he'd just done. He turned and shone his torch onto the wall above The Drop. There was little to see, but clearly something had been different, there had been nowhere for his feet. He glanced up at the light in front of him, he was relieved to see it was still glowing. Sion stumbled to his feet, wiping away a little of the blood from his face with the back of his hand and began to open the door.

Sion hadn't considered how awful he might have looked, until Geoff saw him. The welcoming smile on Geoff's face had turned to a look of complete horror within a second of them making eye contact. Geoff rushed towards Sion and ushered him down the steps and into his front room. Tarquin, who had been sitting across two of Geoff's dining chairs, stood and rushed over towards Sion, banging his head on a shimmering, antique chandelier, as Geoff disappeared into the kitchen, only to return moments later with a lady, presumably his wife.

"Sion, this is my wife Katla," Geoff began. "She'll get you all cleaned up. Come with me."

Sion followed Geoff and Katla to the kitchen, where he was given a stool, before having the blood, rather roughly, wiped from his face and a plaster (of sorts) put onto his forehead.

"So," began Tarquin with a visible smirk, "you didn't remember what I said about the ledge then?"

"Er," Sion stammered, "no. Well, I don't remember seeing anything about it."

"It was at the end of my last email, but never mind. You're ok and you made it," Tarquin continued. "Now, let's all have a cup of tea. There's lots to discuss."

"Go and find some seats gentlemen," Katla said as she shepherded them back into the lounge, "I'll get the kettle on."

Tarquin returned to his two dining chairs, rubbing at his own, slightly less injured head, while Geoff steered Sion towards the floral armchair, by the fireplace, before perching himself on the matching footstool. After a few moments of silence, Katla returned to the room with a tray of steaming tea and homemade biscuits.

Still shaking slightly from his ordeal, Sion sipped his tea and patted at his plaster-topped wound. It throbbed and was definitely still bleeding a little, as the plaster was damp.

"Don't fiddle with it, poppet," Katla whispered across to him. "It'll feel better soon. I'll have another look at it before you go." She gave him a wink with her sparkling blue eyes. She was a very pretty lady. Similar in height to Geoff, but very well dressed. She wore make up and jewellery and had her pristinely manicured fingernails, painted in a glossy silver. As Sion's eyes moved around the room, he caught sight of a photograph on the wall. Presumably from the outfits, it was Geoff and Katla's wedding. The picture seemed to have been taken somewhere icy, as the walls and floor around the pair were white and shiny. Katla had noticed Sion's gaze and began to fill him in.

"That's our wedding. Wonderful day it was. It's an ice cave, back home in Iceland. That's where I'm from. Beautiful place. Have you been?" Katla asked Sion, as he stuffed another biscuit into his mouth.

"No, I haven't. Looks spectacular. Do they have volcanoes too?"

"Oh yes! An awesome sight when they go!"

Placing his empty cup down, a little too roughly, Tarquin turned to Sion. He had been chatting quietly with Geoff for the last few minutes and Sion hadn't made out a single word.

"So, Sion, we've got a lot to discuss. Where should we start?"

"Er," Sion stammered again. "I don't know."

"Well," Tarquin began. "You know enough about the cave at the moment, but there's summat we're going to share with you, as you may be of 'elp, seen as you live locally 'n' that."

Sion's eyes lit up and he sat up straight. This was exciting, he was going to be important and was going to try very hard to do whatever he could.

"You know 'ow the alarm went off last time you were 'ere?" Tarquin continued.

Sion nodded.

"Well, as I mentioned, a vent 'ad been breached and it's not thought to 'av been an accident this time, if you get what I mean."

Sion nodded again, even though he didn't completely understand.

"Someone who was livin' in the caves for many years, maybe tryin' to get back in. They know, see. They know 'ow to do it."

"Why are they trying to come back?" Sion replied. He was unsure too of why they didn't use the main entrance through the cave. They must know it was there.

"Well, they want summut that's 'ere. The found it and they wanna keep it. You know. Get it back like."

"Sorry," Sion hesitantly replied. "But, why don't they try and come in through the cave, like we do?"

"What happens when you come in, Sion?" Tarquin asked, gesturing towards Geoff.

"Oh," Sion realised. "They'd be met at the door."

"Exactly! So they're trying t'use a vent without settin' an alarm off."

"So," Sion continued in his hesitant tone. "If I'm allowed to ask. Why do they no longer live here?"

At this question, Tarquin, Geoff and Katla all glanced at one another with uneasy expressions. With a deep, nasal intake of breath, Geoff began to answer.

"They're fugitive. On the run. A wanted person." Geoff went silent and looked down at the carpet. Katla retrieved some tissue from her sleeve and handed it to Geoff. He wiped his eyes and returned his gaze to Sion's.

"They killed someone," Geoff continued. "It was claimed to be an accident, but I was there and I'll tell you now, it wasn't. Patrice was a great friend and a tremendously hard worker. He was just doing his job." Geoff was visibly struggling to speak now, as Tarquin took over and Katla comforted her husband.

"Well said Geoff," Tarquin reached across and patted Geoff on the back. "Basically Sion, this person needs to be stopped. We need to catch 'em. Get 'em back here to be locked away for what they did." Tarquin was rubbing his sweating hands together as he spoke. "We think that they'll try the same vent again, so we want you to go there, whenever you can. Just to look. I can show you on a map exactly where it is. You can keep a lookout for anythin' changin'. That ok?"

"Yeah, sure. It's near my school, so I could pop over most days, even if just for a few minutes," Sion replied eagerly.

"Great, thanks Sion. I'll email you some more details later today."

Time flew as, a now more composed, Geoff retold anecdotes of his time with Patrice. Eventually Katla stood and ushered Sion into the kitchen for a quick wound check-up. She cleaned off the now drying blood and put a fresh plaster on the cut above his eyebrow. Sion was slightly concerned about what his mother would say on his return. Hopefully she'd not be too alarmed. Before he left, Tarquin gave Sion some advice about how to get back past the overhang without injury, before giving him a hard, yet friendly, pat on the back. It was good advice too, Sion made it across with no trouble.

As he ambled back down the hill, towards his house, he removed the plaster and stuffed it into his pocket. He felt that a wiped wound would be easier to explain than a dressed one. As it happened, he arrived home to an empty house, apart from Albert, who came to give Sion a welcoming lick and sniff. A note under the pepper pot explained that his parents and Gwen were visiting friends and would be back by five o'clock. Sion was pleased to see that it also mentioned a sausage sandwich keeping warm for him. He located the sandwich and a carton of orange juice and made his way upstairs, with Albert close behind him.

Chapter 20

Who Was That?

Returning to school on Monday morning was a mixture of highs and lows for Sion. He always enjoyed catching up with his friends. He'd get to play football. He had science, which he loved. But most of all, he was hoping to make his first visit to the woodland to see if he could find the vent. Tarquin had emailed across an explanation of how to find it, which Sion had printed off and had safely tucked in his trouser pocket. The downside of Monday was, it was RE day, so Sion and his classmates would have the 'delight' of Mrs Anderson for fifty minutes. She'd returned to school last Tuesday. Sion hadn't seen her face to face, but he'd heard another pupil complaining about a detention she'd given him. Trying to be optimistic, Sion kept reminding himself that fifty minutes was not a long time and that the majority of the day would be fine, if not great, in comparison.

When Sion and his classmates arrived at Mrs Anderson's classroom door, she was already sitting behind her desk, staring down at a book. She looked up briefly and called Sion's name, summoning him towards her with her wrinkled index finger.

"Hand these out," she muttered, thrusting a pile of papers into Sion's hand.

As he took the papers, Sion caught a glimpse of her right foot. She was wearing a boot. Velcro strapping wrapped around from toe to knee, with a plaster cast and big toe nail just visible at the end.

"How have you done that, Mrs Anderson?" Sion asked, pointing towards her strapped foot and leg.

"I fell," came the abrupt reply. "Now hand those out, quickly."

Without another thought and wishing he'd not asked, Sion began to distribute the papers, audible groans coming frequently from classmates, as they looked over their sheets.

"When I tell you to start," began Mrs Anderson, still not looking up. "You'll have forty five minutes to complete your sheet. No talking or communicating with anyone and definitely no visits to the toilet. That includes you, Anwen." Mrs Anderson looked up at this point, causing the aforementioned girl to blush uncontrollably, resulting in a few sniggers and giggles. Despite the tedious task, Sion was quite pleased that this was going to be a silent lesson. Not having to actually listen to Mrs Anderson was the silver lining to the test paper cloud.

The time passed quickly and when Mrs Anderson told the class to stop, Sion was almost done. He raised his hand to ask if she'd like him to collect the papers back for her. She nodded in agreement and dismissed the class with a quick motion of her finger towards the door.

Break time was only fifteen minutes, so a quick bit of football and a catch up with the lads was called for, while simultaneously stuffing down a packet of pickled onion Monster Munch. Maths next, which Sion really enjoyed. His teacher was really enthusiastic, bubbly and a bit rude, in a fun way. Mrs Douglas was young, always had new ideas and loved to use the IPads and interactive games in lessons. There was always laughter and you never left the room feeling downbeat or that you couldn't do maths. He was sure the lesson would fly by and that his chance to visit the woodland would soon be upon him.

He was right, after some mental maths challenges, they spent their session doing an online maths quiz in teams, against another school. It had been an exciting draw; the whole class was buzzing as they poured out of Mrs Douglas' room.

Making an excuse about meeting his mother, Sion left school and turned up the footpath towards the woodland. Once he was out of the sight of his friends, he began to jog, while removing his instructions from his trouser pocket. He'd remembered that he had to walk approximately thirty metres into the woods, find a red bin for disposing of dog mess, turn left behind it and continue through the trees to a small pond. Glancing down at the notes, Sion confirmed that he needed to be at the almost other side of the pond. There he should find a large, gnarled oak tree with a mass of roots. Somewhere on those roots he'd find the symbol, the symbol that he'd first seen on Tarquin's skin, what seemed now, like aeons ago. Sion had reached what he presumed was the correct tree, within ten minutes of leaving school. He was pleased. This meant that coming again would not be difficult. He began scouring the roots for the symbol, he was unsure of the size it was going to be and if it was completely hidden. He didn't need to look for long. On the side of a large, arched root, there it was, again about the size of a two pence coin. As Sion moved his fingers towards it, he could actually feel a draft coming from under the marked root. Once again, Sion was filled with a feeling of awe. He knew what that draft was. He knew what was inside. He'd seen it with his own eyes. He wasn't going to tell anyone, but to be fair, he knew that most people wouldn't believe him anyway. It was then that he remembered why he was there. Getting to his feet, Sion looked around the tree for any signs of disturbance. About two metres from the vent, the ground had

clearly been dug and fairly recently too. The leaves and moss, present everywhere else, were missing and were replaced by a mixture of soil and stones, covering about a metre square. Sion prodded the area with a large stick, before pushing it into the soil, to see how far it went down. Without warning, Sion fell into a heap, covering the knees of his school trousers in soil, as the stick disappeared straight through the ground. He fiddled about with his fingers to find it, but it was gone. He found a larger stick and carefully repeated the exercise. Again, the stick went down, but this time Sion held onto the end and pulled it back up, before discarding it cautiously into some nearby grass. For today, that was all Sion could do, he still had plenty to fill Tarquin in with. Stuffing the instructions back into his pocket, Sion made his way back to school, brushing the soil and moss from his knees. There was still just under half of his dinner break left, as he came back through the gates to join his friends, who were just finishing their lunches. Sion wished he could share what he knew with some of them, but he knew he shouldn't, not yet anyway.

Hi Tarquin,

Managed to get to the woodland today, found the vent, I could even feel a draft. Someone has dug a hole in the ground not far from the vent. It's been filled in with soil. I poked it with a stick and it's very deep, I think. I'm going to pop back tomorrow, after school and have another look at it, see if I can work out how deep it goes. Apart from that, I didn't see anything else. No tools or anything out of the ordinary. Will message you again tomorrow if I find out any more.

Sion

In an attempt to work out the depth of the hole, Sion had decided to take some of his dad's strong sticking tape that was usually used for holding broken, plastic pipes together or similar. He'd get hold of several strong sticks of a good length, tape them together, work out their approximate total length before trying the hole again. It'd give him an idea. Hopefully, the soil would still be soft and dry enough to poke the stick through, it wasn't forecast to rain. On a Tuesday, Sion's mother was always late collecting him, about twenty minutes later. Usually, he'd just hang about, people watching or cowering from the horizontal rain, under the almost useless school bus shelter, with its roof and side panels partially missing. He'd have plenty of time to pop back to the tree, stick the sticks together and test the hole's depth. Even if his mother was waiting for him on his return, it was a footpath, he liked walking, nothing suspicious about that.

So, after an ordinary day at school, with his ordinary friends, doing his ordinary lessons, Sion went to pursue his extraordinary task once more. It hadn't rained, but it was cold, hopefully not too cold to make the ground hard. Sion arrived at the tree quickly and set to work looking for suitable sticks, it wasn't hard, there were plenty. He sat on a patch of dry earth, the area around him festooned in leaves of every autumnal shade. The industrial tape was hard to rip or tear, as is its purpose, so Sion gnawed at it with his teeth, as he added each stick. As the last stick was attached, Sion estimated that he'd done between four and five metres. Looking at the dug area, it didn't seem quite the same as yesterday. It was still obviously different from the area around it, but there was less soil, more leaves and twigs. Sion prepared his elongated stick and began to push it into the hole. Within a second, it had hit something. He raised it and tried again a few centimetres away. Once again, the stick was met with an obstacle. Sion put his stick down and lowered to his knees to examine the hole. He brushed at the leaves, twigs and soil with his hand and exposed something flat and wooden. Brushing away more of the tree debris, it was clear that the deep, freshly dug hole from yesterday was now covered with a large piece of wood and whoever had put it there, was keen to keep it hidden. He'd never have seen it, had he not wiped the top clear. Sion jumped to his feet as a snap of a twig sounded behind him. His heart racing, he looked all around, but saw no one. A grey squirrel was leaping fearlessly from branch to branch above his head, maybe that's who was responsible. Glancing around again, feeling a little foolish for his fear, Sion returned to his knees. He tried to move the board, but it was well packed in with earth, it would be a longer job, something that he'd need to return for. He covered it back over as best as he could and threw his taped stick creation into the bushes, his mother would be there waiting any minute now. As he came back down the path and out on the pavement by the bus stop, he could see his mother's car approaching the school layby.

Tarquin had been working away on a removal job in Scotland most of the week, so had only given Sion a brief reply. Congratulating him for his continued work and inviting him to return to Geoff and Katla's on Saturday as they were going to give him a tour of the main cave area. This excited Sion, even stopped him sleeping. The cave had been so incredibly exciting the first time he set foot in it. The size, the glow worms, the noises. Due to a change in the weather, mid-week, Sion did not return to the woods before the weekend. It had been bitterly cold and the rain and wind were some of the worst Sion had seen. He had explained to Tarquin, who didn't seem too bothered. Thankfully, by Saturday morning, the storm conditions had eased. There was a gentle breeze and sporadic drizzle, but nothing to stop Sion bouncing out of bed, dressing and leaving the house by eight o'clock. Once again, he told his parents that he'd be home before lunch, to give himself plenty of time. He did not want to miss a second of this visit, he couldn't begin to imagine what he might see or who he might meet.

Getting past The Drop was a challenge again, but at least this time Sion was expecting the lack of footing and he made it across quickly. Geoff was waiting for him at the door and was noticeably relieved to see that this time, Sion was not sporting a blood-stained face.

"Good morning, Sion," Geoff greeted, as he bounded towards him for a handshake. "How're you today? I'm really looking forward to giving you a proper tour of my home and introducing you to some friends."

"I can't wait!" Sion said, struggling to contain an excited squeak in his voice.

"Come. Let's have a cup of tea first." Geoff took hold of Sion's arm and encouraged him towards his door. Sion was not thrilled by the delay to his tour, but he was keen to be polite and courteous, so without complaint, he followed Geoff in. Tarquin was waiting inside on his double dining chair seat, chatting to Katla, who was pouring out tea.

"Sion, m'boy!" Tarquin got to his feet and gave Sion one of his pats on the back that almost knocked him to the ground. "Well done with the vent work. Really impressed. You're a dedicated lad, I can see. Definitely worth a trip next week please, see if anyone 'as moved it again. We think they're tryin' to get into the vent pipes, see. They know what they're doin'. Very crafty. Very crafty. Anyway, drink yer brew and we'll show yer 'round."

Sion didn't join in much with the conversation over tea. Tarquin and Geoff were roaring with laughter at another cave dweller's expense. It seemed that someone they both knew had put on a bit too much weight and had become wedged in a vent pipe while cleaning out leaves. Sion felt a bit sorry for whoever this was, but could see why his companions were so amused, it probably was funny for everyone else.

"Right then Sion, you finished?" Geoff sprang to his feet and skipped towards the door. Sion was pleased that Tarquin hadn't done the same. He'd have slammed into the ceiling, again.

"Have a wonderful time!" Katla called after them, as they set off through the door.

Sion turned and waved to her, beaming from ear to ear, he couldn't remember a time when he'd felt more excited and he didn't even know what he was going to see.

Chapter 21

What is Glowing?

Outside Geoff and Katla's door the path ran towards the entrance, up the steps on the right and down to the floor of the main cave on the left. A rope barrier was all that prevented a fall from the path to the floor, a fall of at least forty metres. The cave ceiling was closer, in comparison, probably only about ten metres above Sion's head. The countless glow worms that gave light to the cave, were dotted around the ceiling and the far side. Now he had time to look, Sion could see that there were at least another five homes along the top path, by Geoff and Katla's. All with an intricately decorated wooden door and a pull-chain doorbell. Each door also had an arched leaded window pane with their own decorative stained glass insert. As they made their way down the steep path, towards the cave floor, Sion saw that as well as the glow worms, there were a few chandelier type lamps dimly lighting the way. The path was slippery, so the rope gave Sion some much needed stability during their descent. For a large man, Tarquin was surprisingly steady on his feet, not slipping or holding the rope, probably because he had been so many times before. As expected, Geoff almost skipped down the path with the confidence of a mountain goat. Sion was relieved to get his feet onto the flat floor at the foot of the path. He raised his head and surveyed the vast space above him. It was more incredible than he'd expected. He felt suddenly insignificant, like one drop of rain in a cloud, one ice crystal in a glacier. He tried to count the twinkling glow worms above him, flickering like stars in the night sky.

"Beautiful ain't it?" Tarquin whispered. "Do you think you could count 'em?"

"No. I don't think I could."

"So," Geoff said, clapping his hands together and making Sion jump. "You're suitably impressed with the cave here?"

"It's wonderful, Geoff. Thank you for bringing me down here."

"Well, this is not the end of your tour. If you're impressed with this cave, I'm confident that you'll want to move on." Geoff motioned Sion to follow him, leading him towards a small wooden door. Sion wasn't sure that Tarquin would even fit through, a concern that Tarquin himself didn't seem to have. The door was similar to Geoff's own front door, but smaller still, it had no window and only limited carved decoration. Geoff pulled a large key from his pocket and unlocked the door with a clunk that echoed around the cave walls behind them. He turned to Sion.

"You're about to see something that only a handful of people like you (he gestured towards Sion and Tarquin), have seen before, Tarquin being one of them. It is likely that you'll be open-mouthed for a time. This is my work and my life and you must NEVER speak of what you've seen. Do you understand, Sion?" Geoff spoke firmly, but still had his friendly tone and a glisten in his eye. Sion nodded, not quite sure what he could say, apart from just agreeing with him. He looked around at Tarquin, whose eyes were welling up with tears.

"What's the matter?" Sion whispered, suddenly concerned.

"It's just the most wonderful sight, Sion. It'll take your breath away, it will."

If this giant of a man was moved to tears, there must be something spectacular behind this rather unassuming wooden door. As Geoff pushed the handle, Sion held his breath and closed his eyes.

Chapter 22

Can Minds Literally Be Blown?

In the split second before he opened his eyes to the sight before him, Sion was startled by the sound of water. Rushing water and lots of it. The spectacle he saw did leave him open-mouthed, as Geoff had predicted. The cave in front of him dwarfed the one behind, so much so that Sion couldn't see the other side. This cave would fit at least twenty of the other one in, no problem. It was colossal. Standing on the steps and looking out reminded Sion of the footage he'd seen of the daredevil Felix Baumgartner, prior to his live parachute jump from space. A magnificent waterfall on Sion's right was gushing from the ceiling down to the floor and down through an opening to a cave below. An enormous waterwheel turned nearby, as the free flowing water poured over it. Hundreds of seemingly busy people were dashing about wherever he looked. Glancing around to the left, Sion could see that the walls were lined with hundreds of shining gates, some of which you could make out something behind them.

"What are the gates for?" Sion whispered to Geoff.

"Each gate protects a different artefact, Sion. There are over a thousand of them. Each person has a gate chamber to look after, as well as other jobs of course. What do you think?"

"Er, I don't know what to say," Sion stammered slightly. "It's like a dream. I can't believe this is here and no one knows."

"The thing you need to remember too, Sion, is that none of what you see is make believe or magical. These are real people, small granted, but real people doing a real job in a real place. No sorcery, no tricks."

Sion could hear Tarquin sniffing behind him.

"Well said, Geoff. It just blows my mind, Sion. Blows my mind," Tarquin muttered through sniffs.

"Do you want to come down and meet some friends, Sion? Maybe have a look through a few gates. I can show you my gate. I share it with Maurice. Lovely chap. Likes a practical joke though, so be prepared for a wind up, if he's in the mood." Geoff led Sion and Tarquin down a set of steep stone steps that zigzagged from the path by the door to the floor of the cave. They must have gone down at least two hundred steps by the time they reached the bottom. Sion had attempted to count them initially, but decided to concentrate more on where he was putting his feet.

Clearly, not everyone knew Tarquin, as there were some startled faces as the man twice the size of most cave dwellers landed at the bottom. Not a minute after their arrival at ground level, Geoff was introducing Sion to someone.

"Sion, this is Maurice, my co-worker." Maurice held out a hand, which Sion shook politely. Maurice wore mostly brown, with a beige and brown checked shirt. His sandalled feet seemed large for his petit frame, or so Sion thought.

"Follow me Sion and Tarquin of course. I'll show you where Geoff and I work. How do you like the cave? Bet you've not seen the like before."

"No I definitely haven't," Sion replied, still scrutinising his surroundings.

Geoff and Maurice led Sion and Tarquin to a row of gates on the first floor level, up ten large stone steps. Their gate had the number 1649 engraved in a metal plaque at the top. The double gates were an arch in shape and golden or brass-like in colour, similar in height to Geoff and Maurice. Sion stooped and tried to peer inside, he couldn't see anything specific. Maurice took a match from his trouser pocket, struck it on the wall and reached inside the gate to light a candle. In the middle of the opening, on a rock, sat a golden tiara or necklace with a selection of large stones at the front which sparkled in the glow from the candle.

"Wow," Sion uttered. "What's that?"

"It's a diadem," Maurice began. "It is believed to be from King Charles the first of England's crown jewels."

Sion glanced up at the number on the door again.

"Yes, Sion. The number is significant. That is the year that Charles was executed. Unless it's of an unknown age, the artefacts here will be numbered based on their age or when they were obtained. This precious piece would've been destroyed, like the rest of his crown jewels, but thankfully, we acquired it, just in time."

"Destroyed by whom? Oh, Cromwell?" Sion felt a little smug for remembering such things.

"Yes. Goodness, well done for knowing that. Very impressive. I can see why Geoff likes you."

Sion looked at his watch, it was already gone ten o'clock. He could stay there all day and learn more and more, there was so much to take in, but he must get back home in time, or his parents would be sending out a search party for him. There was one more thing that he wanted to know before he left though.

"Geoff, where is the item that the person wants to get back? Is it near here?"

"Yes, it's two floors up. Would you like to see it?"

"Yes please, if that's alright."

"It's fine, we'll pop up to show you, then get you back in time to go home. You can always come back again." Geoff leaned across and blew out the candle, plunging the hollow and diadem into darkness once more.

Another steep climb up two flights of stone steps and the party of four arrived at another row of gates, identical to the row they'd just seen. Once again, Maurice struck a match and reached inside to light a small candle. This time upon a similarly large stone was a much larger object. A sword. Not gleaming with jewels or encrusted in gold, just a sword with some engravings near the top of the blade.

"Whose is this?" Sion asked, glancing up at the number.

"1792. This is the sword of Joan of Arc."

"Wasn't Joan of Arc alive much earlier than 1792?" Sion questioned further.

"Yes. Well done again. However, the sword was acquired during the revolution in France, so the number reflects that, not the age of the sword itself."

"So, why does this person want to get hold of the sword?" Sion continued, forgetting about his limited time to get home.

"It's a long story Sion, too long for now," Geoff answered, sighing slightly. "I'll fill you in with more soon. They just want it as they think it's their property, which of course it isn't and we must all do everything we can to make sure it stays here, where it belongs. If just one of these treasures were to get back out, chances are, in time, we'd be discovered and then that would be that. Millennia of work gone."

"Well said Geoff," murmured Tarquin from behind Sion.

With that, Geoff encouraged Sion towards some more steps up.

"We'll go this way. Come on, let's get you home."

The trio of visitors left Maurice outside cave number 1792. Sion turned to wave as Maurice blew out the candle. Maurice gave Sion a wink and waved back before making his way back down to his own gates. The steps up were exhausting and by the time they arrived at the path to the door, Sion and Tarquin were both puffing and panting like overworked dogs. Geoff unlocked the door once more, leading Sion and Tarquin through before relocking it. Once again, the noise of the lock sent an echo bouncing around the cave walls. This cave seemed so small and paltry now in comparison.

"No time for more tea, have we?" enquired Geoff, rubbing his palms together, as they reached the pathway outside his door.

"I best not, but thank you. It's been the most incredible morning, Geoff. I'm going to try my very best to help in any way I can. I'll go back to the woodland on Monday and will report back."

Sion gave Geoff and Tarquin a wave and let himself out of the door and into the cave entrance. He pressed the light on his watch. Just past eleven o'clock. He was an expert at The Drop now and made it to the other side in less than a minute. Before leaving the cave, Sion sat down for a moment to digest what he'd just seen and what he knew. His tummy rumbled. Time to return to normality and eat lunch. Sion left the cave and skidded down the hill, through the kissing gate and in through the back door.

Chapter 23

Will I Find it?

The clock in Sion's room ticked relentlessly as he lay awake, seeing in every hour of the night. Darkness turning to dawn. A resident wood pigeon sent harmonious communication to his friends in the trees that surrounded the house. As dawn turned to daylight, more birdsong was joined by the muffled movements of Sion's family, as they began morning journeys to bathroom and kettle. Still Sion lay still. He was certain that he'd not slept all night. His mind had been on fire with thoughts. Images and considerations whirred around his head like traffic navigating Spaghetti Junction. His eyes had frequently widened as some of these thoughts passed through. Yesterday he'd seen just two of over a thousand chambers inside that cave. He'd met just one other cave dweller, out of thousands of diligent workers, all with one goal; to keep their artefacts safe and secure. Unconscious in thought, the knock at the door brought Sion back like a shot of adrenaline.

"Cup of tea, Sion?" his mother said in an enquiring tone, even though she was already placing the cup on his table. "I'll just open your curtains. You sleep well? Don't forget we need to be out by nine at the latest. Could you take Albert for a quick walk when you're up? He needs to do business before getting in the car for two hours."

She hadn't really given an opportunity to answer any of her questions, so Sion just agreed to the Albert part and ignored the sleep enquiry. He had forgotten about the trip out today, it hadn't even entered his mind over the last few days. Visiting aunts and uncles wasn't really what Sion wanted to spend his Sunday doing. He contemplated asking his mother if he could stay at home, but after thinking it through once, he decided against it. She would not be happy, especially as he'd got out of the last visit too. Pulling on a hoodie and wedging himself upright with pillows, Sion sipped at his hot tea and gazed out of his window. He still didn't know who the other person had been, whom he'd seen by the cave a few weeks ago. That question joined the vat of other questions tumbling around, inside his head. He needed to freshen up, get his brain in gear. A quick walk with Albert and a shower should sort him out. That and a bacon sandwich. He'd seen the bacon last night. His father always liked to make everyone a bacon and egg bap before they went on a journey and also on Christmas Day morning. They were known in Sion's house as 'Murphy breakfasts'. Named after a construction company, whom Sion's father had worked for many years ago. Apparently the bacon and egg bap was the breakfast of champions, as far as his colleagues had been concerned.

As predicted, as Sion plodded down the stairs, his father called to him.

"Murphy breakfast, Sion?"

"Just taking Albert out then having a shower. Would love one in twenty minutes. That ok?"

His father's call of agreement came as Sion slammed the back door shut. Albert was very keen to go out and led Sion towards their usual route. Through/over the kissing gate, through the field, up the track, past the cave and back down. He needed to be quick this morning, but Sion popped into the cave for a glance around. Nothing to be seen. He turned to leave.

"Mornin' fella. Goodness, that's a dog and an 'alf."

Sion knew that he hadn't contained the terrified jump or squeak of alarm.

"Good morning," Sion replied, making haste to leave. "Yes, this is Albert. He's a Great Dane."

The stranger gave Albert a rub between the ears, which was gratefully accepted. Sion might have been apprehensive, but Albert was just fine with anyone, who knew where to scratch. Sion stepped out into the light again and looked up at the man's face. He was certain it was the man he'd seen from his house. Tall, but slimmer and a little shorter than Tarquin. He had a stubbly chin and piercingly blue eyes. He wore a long, dark wax jacket with green wellington boots and had a dark-tan Stetson style hat, a long, brown feather protruding from its side.

"Well it's nice to meet you, Sion. See y'round." He turned away from Sion and Albert, leaving Sion speechless for a split second.

"How do you know my name?" Sion asked, trying to sound more confident than he was.

"Knew I'd bump into you at some point. I'm Terrance, but Terry'll do. You know me mate, Quinny, don't yer?"

Relief rushed through Sion's body.

"Oh! Yes, I do," Sion began, glancing down at his watch. "Nice to meet you, Terry. I'm sorry, I'm going to have to dash off. My parents are waiting for me to bring Albert back."

"No problem, Sion. See yer 'round."

With that, Sion galloped back down the path with Albert bounding just ahead of him. Looking back up at the cave, he could see Terry disappearing inside. He smiled. It felt good to have met someone else who apparently knew. Like sharing the burden of a weighty secret.

After a shower and a 'Murphy breakfast', Sion was feeling as fresh as a daisy. Sure, the lack of sleep would catch up with him, but right now, he was buoyant. He'd had another thought too. The family were off to the heart of the Staffordshire countryside. There'd probably be a vent near where they were going. Maybe Sion could try to find it while walking Albert. He rushed off upstairs to scour the map Tarquin had given him and sure enough, about ten minutes' walk from the village they were visiting, there was a vent. Once again, it seemed to be a wooded area. That was his challenge for today sorted, should keep him occupied during the inevitably tiresome visit.

During the journey down, Sion pretended to do some homework. It was homework of sorts, just not from school. Gwen wasn't remotely interested in what Sion was doing. She was experimenting with a hairstyle and make-up app on her tablet. Occasionally, Sion would glance across and snigger at her selfie creations and exaggerated pouting. Gwen's current style of choice was watered down Goth. Dark hair, unlike her mousy brown, with lots of intricate makeup. She'd even started listening to what she considered to be rock music. It wasn't rock music, by definition. It was teeny bop bands who happened to have guitars. Sion doubted that they could even play them. She shot him a glare as he sniggered again at the purple lipstick she'd added to her picture. In contrast, Sion was compiling a list of questions and thoughts that he wanted or needed to know more about. People to meet, things to see, places to visit. He felt like a spy, a secret agent whom no one knew about. His family, who were seated around him right now, had no idea about the clandestine cave network that he'd been visiting or the thousands of people inhabiting it.

"Here we are," Sion's mother announced as the handbrake creaked. "Sion, wake up!"

"What?" Sion muttered, wiping a trickle of dribble from his chin. "I am awake."

He'd been dozing for some time, his neck was stiff. He stretched himself as far as he could in the back seat, while everyone else greeted the awaiting aunt. Albert had been released from the boot and was on his back legs, pinning Sion's uncle to the wall in an attempt to lick his face.

"Down Albert, down!" Sion's mother scolded. "You'll be back in that boot!"

Lunch with Uncle John and Aunty Emily was always the same. Delicious buffet style lunch, but tedious and predictable conversation, often concerning family who were currently not speaking to one another. Aunty Emily always had an opinion and was keen to share it. Sion was happy to sit and focus on the spread of food. After every visit, Aunty Emily would always make them a bag up of the leftovers, which Sion and Gwen would graze on for days after. Today was going to be no exception. There was a hand-raised pork pie with its thick layer of jelly, warm new potatoes in melted butter, a variety of crust-less sandwiches on soft white bread, rolled up Staffordshire oatcakes with bacon and cheese oozing from the edges and an ornate, cut-glass bowl full of cherry tomatoes and cucumber sticks. Goodness knows what would appear for the sweet. Aunty Emily liked to make Eton Mess or trifle. Sion remembered Gwen eating too much of Aunty Emily's sherry trifle, one Christmas. She'd spent the next day in bed with a headache. Sion's father had been convinced that she had a hangover from its alcohol content.

As Uncle John cleared away the plates and gave Albert a ham sandwich, Aunty Emily returned to the dining room with her creation. An enormous pavlova. Meringue discs, almost the size of car wheels, sandwiched together with lashings of whipped cream, fresh strawberries and raspberries and showered in grated chocolate.

"Wow, Aunty Emily!" Sion's mother spoke, as everyone else just stared agog.

It was during the pudding course that Sion decided to ask how far the woods were from the house.

"If you turn right out of drive," began Uncle John, "go two hundred yards down pavement and then take a right over stile. Across the field there and it'll take you 'bout ten minutes. You taking pooch out? We can all go. Good constitutional. Do us all good like."

Everyone nodded in agreement, apart from Gwen who was far too concerned about her pavlova to notice. Albert had noticed. The 'taking pooch out' remark had alerted him to a possible walk and he'd begun visiting everyone in turn, around the table. Sniffing and nudging at them.

Aunty Emily opted to stay behind to clean up and organise their 'doggy bag', but Uncle John enthusiastically pulled on his boots and jacket. Clearly he didn't get out walking as much as he'd like.

He'd been spot on with the directions and timing, despite their slow post-lunch pace, they arrived at the trees within about fifteen minutes of leaving the house. Sion wasn't convinced that he'd find the vent in the time that he had, they were so small, but it was giving him something other than indigestion to think about. He presumed that it'd be 'labelled' in the same way, with the mark he now knew so well. But it would be small, very hard to see without crouching down. He scoured the trees around him for root networks, somewhere likely. A lot of the trees were conifers or birch, both bending and swaying in the breeze and less likely locations for vents. Sion was looking for something more substantial, an oak, sycamore or horse chestnut tree that'd stood for a century or more.

After tramping around the woods for nearly half an hour, Sion spotted a good specimen. A wide trunked oak with plenty of bulging roots. Pleasingly, Albert seemed keen to sniff around this tree, particularly around one part. Sion looked around at his family, who were all happily chatting and walking. He knelt down and scrutinised the roots with his eyes and fingers. A draught, he felt it and sure enough there on the underside of the root was the etched mark. You'd never see it if you didn't know.

Sion panicked slightly when he noticed Albert doing one of his everlasting wees against the side of the tree. Hopefully, it wouldn't pour into the cave. That would be embarrassing.

"What you seen, Sion?" called his father.

"Oh nothing, just thought I saw a mouse."

"Has Albert done any business yet?"

"Just a wee."

On their arrival back at the house, Aunty Emily had made a much appreciated pot of tea. No one touched the chintz plate of biscuits. They were still bursting at the seams from lunch.

Sion, Gwen, their parents and Albert set off for home with their bag of leftovers. It'd been an enjoyable day. Of course, Sion would've liked to have been back at the cave, meeting new people and finding out more, but he'd found another vent and had really enjoyed his lunch. Tomorrow he'd go back to school and back to 'work'.

Chapter 24

Who's Trying to Kill Me?

With a Monday, came the monotony of Mrs Anderson's RE lesson. With leg strapping still in place, she sat in the classroom awaiting her victims, just as she'd done the previous week. On entering the room with their sullen looks and dragging feet, Sion and his classmates took their regular seats. Another of Mrs Anderson's quibbles had been that, "Students must not move to new spaces! Pick one and stick with it!"

Even by her own dismal standards, Mrs Anderson was not omitting any enthusiasm. Books were distributed, a page number given and a brief instruction about reading, answering the questions and copying the diagram were muttered. While Sion and his classmates were beavering away in silence, Mrs Anderson spent the session writing into a notebook and occasionally looking up. Sion had made eye contact with her on one of these glances upward. After this, his gaze never moved above the nibbled rim of his desk, even during the final ten minutes, while he waited, jaded, staring at the page number in the corner of his textbook. Someone had previously coloured in the nine and drawn a line to join the seven's top and bottom, so ninety seven was now an apostrophe and a right-angled triangle. Sion contemplated if any other page numbers could be amusing pictures or shapes, if you coloured them carefully. The bell sounded and Sion jumped back to consciousness.

"Of you go," Mrs Anderson almost inaudibly spoke. "Books on my desk. Textbooks away. Chairs under. LIFT THEM!"

Someone had dared to push their chair under. Its shrill jarring cutting through the silence. Before anything else could be said or any detentions given, everyone had rapidly scarpered from the room.

As the lunchtime bell rang at the end of his next lesson, Sion squinted out of the window to check the weather. It was drizzling. He had brought his coat, so he hurried off through the gates, stuffing his sandwich into his mouth. This was going to be a very quick visit, the persistent drizzle had made the woodland floor muddy. The autumn leaves had, all but a few, fallen and combined with the damp weather, were now carpeting the floor with a rotting mush that squelched underfoot. Sion dodged the puddles, slipping once or twice on hidden roots, almost losing his composure. As he approached the vent at almost a jog, he ground to a halt. Next to the tree he could see a brownish green tarpaulin sheet, covering a pile of something. It was on the opposite side of the tree from the path, so you'd never notice it, if you weren't looking there. Sion looked around. This path was used, so there was always the chance of meeting someone. He wasn't quite sure what he'd say if he did meet a stranger walking their dog. A lone teenage boy in the woods during school hours was a little out of the ordinary. Sion checked his watch. He'd have a quick look under the sheet and then go back to school. He could come back later, he was getting a bus back today. He looked around again. No one. Sion edged closer, looking around once more. He looked up into the tree's branches above him. No one. He cautiously lifted the corner of the tarpaulin, a puddle of rain water poured from a dip in the sheet and onto the floor. A little higher he lifted it, until he caught a glimpse of what was hidden. A little higher. Sion got to his knees, the boggy ground soaked his school trousers within seconds, reverting him back to crouching unsteadily on his feet. A shovel, a long, hollow metal pole and a pot of paint. No brushes to paint with, just paint. Sion returned the tarpaulin to its original position and himself upright to his feet. He was a little baffled. A shovel made sense. Even the metal pole could, but paint. Why paint? It was after half past twelve, in just under three hours, Sion would return and see if anything had changed. He'd then email Tarquin when he got home.

The afternoon sped past. Sion and the majority of his year group spent the two hour session doing PE. Ball skills and an indoor five a side football tournament. A heavenly afternoon in Sion's opinion, to contrast to the lacklustre start to the morning. As was often the case, they did not get a chance to change back into their uniforms, so the students were dismissed for the day wearing their PE kits. Sion was glad of his school hoodie and jogging bottoms, he'd have risked hypothermia if he'd returned to the woods in shorts. It really was a bitterly cold autumn day, the breeze wasn't strong, but nipped at your extremities.

Sion chatted for a while to friends as one by one they caught buses or were collected. Sion could've caught the bus with Rhys, but made an excuse about meeting his mother off the next one. By three thirty five, Sion was alone at the bus stop. He'd even watched most of the teachers drive out of the staff car park. The PE teacher, Mr Hughes, had beeped and waved to Sion on his way out. Presumably he was giving extra kudos for the volley Sion had scored earlier. It was a moment of brilliance.

The drizzle had abated as Sion strode up the path. Before he'd even left the well-trodden track, he froze before darting quickly behind another large tree that stood nearby. He peered around the trunk. Dressed in a dark coloured mackintosh that went past the knee, there was a person removing the tarpaulin from the objects he'd seen earlier, the gaping hood of the coat covered their face almost entirely. Sion looked again, this time for a little longer. The person had now removed the items from by the tree and had begun to slide the board away from the hole. Still looking, strangely confident of not being seen, Sion watched as the person dug away at the ground, carefully depositing the leaf matter and soil into a pile behind them. Still looking. Sion was not sure if this person was male or female. He'd expected them to be small and they were. Probably a similar height to Geoff, Katya and Maurice and all other cave dwellers he'd seen. Still looking. The hooded figure suddenly lifted their head and looked around. Sion's head darted back behind the tree where he stood motionless. His breathing seemed deafening. He was focussing so hard on not making a sound that he felt like he could faint, right there and then. He listened. Nothing. Sion's courage returned to him and he gradually turned his head and body to gain one last look. Too soon. The shovel was thrown to the ground and the pole picked up. As Sion made a dash for the path, he turned to see the pole being sent through the air towards him like a javelin. The pole caught the top of Sion's right ear, before hitting a tree ahead of him. He turned again. The figure was now setting off after him, but within seconds had fallen to the ground, most probably stumbling on a tree root. Sion accelerated, leaping over roots, splashing into mud and dodging saplings on the path, slowing only as the road came into view. He touched his ear and examined his fingers. Blood. Again. He turned again. No one. He was prepared for a sudden appearance from the bushes, but to his relief, nothing came. There was still no one in sight as Sion checked the time. He'd got a few minutes until the bus was expected. Sitting on the cold concrete floor of the bus shelter, he took his beanie hat from his bag, turned it inside out and put it on to cover his injured ear. He didn't often wear this hat as it had an England flag on the front and generally resulted in (not always) friendly banter. Sion's heart was still thumping, like it was knocking on his chest door to be let out. He opened his now almost flat lemonade from his bag and finished it. As the bus appeared in the distance, Sion checked the footpath once more. Nothing.

Chapter 25

Will I Always be Scared?

Nausea and adrenaline came in alternate waves, after his escape. He was trying to come to terms with the fact that he'd nearly been killed. Three or four centimetres to the left and he'd have been a goner, harpooned by a rusty metal pole. He thought for a moment that he was going to vomit. Breathing deeply and trying to focus on anything stationary, he collected himself once more. Despite it being a ten minute car trip, the bus journey home took nearly an hour as the route took them around winding lanes and through tiny villages. Sion was glad of the extended sit down, it'd give him time to calm down before getting home. He decided that he'd show his mum his ear and explain that he caught it on the broken bus shelter.

The bus stop wasn't far from his house, about a five minute walk. Unsteady on his feet and still feeling slightly queasy, Sion shuffled to his front door. His face was pale which had alarmed his mother as he entered the kitchen. She hurried towards him and pulled a chair out, which he promptly landed on. He pulled off his hat and pointed at his frayed ear, still not speaking a word, for fear of being sick. Eventually, Sion began to answer his mother's questions and gave her his patter about the bus shelter. He did a good job, she accepted the story, but was adamant that she'd be making a complaint. Maybe that wouldn't be a bad thing, they needed a new shelter.

Gwen was less than impressed that Sion was allowed his dinner in his room. She'd examined his ear and didn't feel that it warranted any special treatment. Their mother disagreed and brought Sion his steaming plate of chicken korma and rice on a tray with a glass of chocolate milkshake for him to have in bed. He'd not emailed Tarquin, but he wasn't yet ready to relive the post-school events. His stomach still turned every time he visualised the pole skimming his head, he'd then become suddenly more mindful of the throbbing from his ear, like a second heartbeat. He wasn't sure if this would pass and allow him to contact Tarquin tonight. He must. What if his lack of correspondence resulted in a breach? Nauseous or not, he had to send that email tonight. His now cleared plate and tray were swapped with his laptop.

Tarquin,

I don't know where to start. I'm alive. Going to keep this short as I'm really not feeling good. Went twice. First time there were things there; a shovel, a pole and paint. Went back later, someone was there, in a cloak or long coat. They saw me and threw the pole. It cut my ear. I'm home now. What should I do?

Sion

He closed his eyes and breathed deeply once more. He was finding it impossible to comprehend that he could've been dead. He could still be lying on the dank floor of the woods, bugs and birds investigating his body. His parents wouldn't know where he was. People would've been searching. And then someone would've found him. The image of his distraught mother appeared in his head and he began to cry. Everything had been so exciting, so exhilarating. Until now. This was intolerable, the feeling of 'what if'.

Feet sounded on the stairs. His door opened slowly. Sion discreetly wiped the tears from his cheeks, but she'd seen and returned the tray to the floor.

"What's the matter darling? Anything you want to tell me?"

"No, I'm ok. I've just got a banging headache."

He wasn't lying, he did have a headache, right behind the eyes. His mother disappeared briefly to fetch some pain killers, which Sion swallowed with the dregs of his milkshake.

"Now, try and get some rest. Think we'll keep you off tomorrow. Maybe you're a bit concussed. I'll ring school in the morning."

Sion hadn't the energy to challenge his mother on the issue, switching off the light as she left the room. He felt dazed. He couldn't even bring himself to check his laptop for a reply. Sion lay slumped in his bed, each tick of his clock felt like a hammer striking a nail further and further into his head.

Chapter 26

Are These My Closest Friends?

"Argh!"

Sion shot upright, flinging his duvet to the floor. Sweating profusely and panic stricken, he scrutinised his room in the dim light of the moon, which seeped around the edges of his heavy, fabric curtains. Relief began to flood back through his veins, as the realisation that the horror he'd just witnessed had been a nightmare. His heart began to race once more when the events of yesterday suddenly re-entered his mind. His nightmare had been similar, but the cloaked figure had caught up with him in the dream version. As they'd grabbed at him from behind, Sion had woken. He thought about his email to Tarquin, but still couldn't bring himself to look for a reply. If he was at home today, as his mother had suggested, maybe he'd feel up to it later on. 03.23 was illuminated on his bedside clock. He reached for his duvet, it was damp with sweat, he'd obviously been in quite a state. Turning the duvet around, he sank back into his bed and tried to think about something, anything else. He tried to visualise the football game and his volley. He imagined doing a lap of the Anfield pitch, crowds cheering, team mates leaping onto him. Then out of nowhere, the hooded figure ran onto the pitch and began to chase him, wielding the rusty pole. Sion tossed and turned, trying desperately to remove the extra character from his thoughts. It was no use. Everything he thought of, no matter how exuberant he was, there they were. By 04.49, Sion had given up. He skulked down the stairs, filled the kettle and opened a packet of digestive biscuits. There wasn't much on the television, worth watching at five o'clock in the morning. Sion settled on a repeat of DIY SOS. Albert had joined him on the sofa, not that he was supposed to get onto the furniture. Sion didn't really care right now. Albert was warm and comforting, like a giant hairy hot water bottle. As long as he kept off the digestives, he could stay put. He stroked Albert's velvety ear and rested his head on the arm of the sofa.

"Get off! Albert down! Off! How many of these did you eat?"

Sion was woken by his mother questioning a guilty looking Albert, whose muzzle was covered in crumbs. He'd nodded off and Albert had taken full advantage.

"How many biscuits had you eaten, Sion?"

"Er, about four, I think."

"Oh great! So Albert's had at least ten chocolate digestives and most of the packaging!"

"Sorry. I must have nodded off. I had a nightmare and couldn't sleep, so I came downstairs."

"Sorry for shouting Sion. How's the head and ear feeling? You going to stay here today, maybe get a nap this afternoon?"

Sion agreed and accepted the offer of another cup of tea in bed. As he lumbered up the stairs, Gwen was running down to get her breakfast.

"Where are you going?" Gwen protested in Sion's direction.

"Bed." Sion shut his door and leaned against it in case she'd followed him. She hadn't, but Sion could now hear Gwen displaying her displeasure in the kitchen below. He saw his laptop as he climbed back into bed. He still wasn't ready to open it. His heart seemed to intermittently race, whenever he thought about anything to do with any of it. Maybe some more sleep and a soak in the bath would improve the anxiety.

His tea arrived. As Sion was buried under a pillow, his mother tiptoed out and closed the door, without a word, presuming he'd nodded off. Sion sat up and sipped at his tea.

He heard his father drive off with Gwen at 08.35. His mother was on hold to the school office, pacing up and down the hall and into the kitchen, shouting, "Oh come on!" every few minutes.

Sion spent the next few hours drifting in and out of sleep. He didn't have another nightmare, although his brain was too tired to think of anything, it would seem. After a soak in near magma heat bath and a bowl of soup with his mother, Sion was feeling better and was able to open his laptop. He sat in his window seat surveying the view. There wasn't much to see. They were in a cloud. He could make out the kissing gate across the road, but no further. Tarquin had responded, he'd kept it succinct.

Sion,

Don't go back please! When can you next get to Geoff's?

Tarquin

Sion replied straight away.

Hi Tarquin,

I won't go back, I promise. Just hope we don't miss anything now. Do you think they'll try again?

I'll try to come up on Saturday. I really can't miss school. Sorry.

Sion

Tarquin was clearly online, as he responded immediately. He explained that he didn't think they'd be trying there again, as the vent had been permanently closed and that Saturday was fine. Sion was already uneasy about going back to the cave, but wasn't sure why. He knew whom he was meeting and the cloaked person was not able to go in that way. The cave was unnerving though, at times you could see virtually nothing, you'd have no idea if you were being watched. Sion shuddered and began talking to himself about being courageous. Regardless of his apprehension, he did feel calmer than he had, so he was back to school for Thursday and Friday. Days that he enjoyed and helped to calm him further, before his trip back to Geoff's on Saturday.

The shrill alarm sounded at 07.00 and Sion stopped it almost instantaneously. He'd been lying awake for at least an hour, thinking about the day's visit. As usual, Sion got up, dressed and out quickly, grabbing a banana as he walked to the door. Albert was eager to go with him, Sion having to prise his paws inside as the door closed. He could hear remonstrating woofs and whines coming from the kitchen, until after he'd crossed the road. Angst circulated Sion's body as he made his way up the hill to the cave entrance and as he stepped into the gloom, his heart beat became increasingly evident to him, he needed all of his composure to get across The Drop in one piece. It had been raining heavily overnight and the sound of dripping and running water was much louder than usual, echoing around Sion like he was inside a waterfall. The extra precipitation had also made the stones very slippery and a large puddle greeted Sion's left foot, as he made the last leap from the ledge to the cave floor on the other side. Squelching, Sion stepped to the door and inside. Geoff was waiting for him, as usual and was once again wearing the Metallica shirt that Sion had seen on his first ever visit, what seemed like years ago. He greeted Sion like a long lost friend, giving him a squeeze and holding his hand as they walked into Geoff's front room together. Tarquin had not arrived yet, but Katla had already prepared her usual pot of tea and plate of biscuits, which Sion was more than happy to begin without Tarquin. Geoff cleared his throat, to prise Sion's attention away from the tea table and onto him.

"Now Sion, when Tarquin gets here, we're going to go through a few things with you. I'm so sorry you had such a bad experience on Tuesday, it's only fair that we fill you in now and let you know our next steps. You know first and second hand that we're dealing with a dangerous person and we all need to be vigilant."

A doorbell sounded.

"I'll go darling," Katla said, darting to the door, "it'll be Tarquin."

Sure enough, seconds later, Tarquin and Katla entered the room, closely followed by Terry. Seeing them together, Sion could see that Terry was much shorter and slighter than his seemingly older brother. He still had to duck down to get in though.

"I've just been saying Quinny," Geoff began, "that we'll give Sion some more information today about all this business. It's only fair. Don't you think?"

"Yeah, I do. Sion, I'm so glad you're ok. You start, tell us what happened."

Sion gave his captivated audience a detailed recount of the events of Tuesday, beginning with his first visit and ending with his injury, escape and thoughts afterwards. No one interrupted him or spoke when he fell silent. Eventually, with a sigh, Terry broke the silence.

"Sion, yer so lucky to be tellin' us about this. I can't stand to think about what could've 'appened. Well done for comin' 'ere and continuin' with us."

"Thanks Terry," Tarquin continued. "Now, Sion, can yer remember anything about what the person looked like? I know yer said yer didn't see a face, but what 'bout build or height? Anythin'."

Sion thought back and imagined the figure in his head.

"Well, they're shorter than me, maybe Geoff's height or even a little shorter still. They seemed slightly bulkier, but it's hard to tell as they could have anything on under the long coat. I couldn't see hair or footwear. Sorry if that's no help. I don't know if it's useful, but when they threw the pole, it was with their left hand and was incredibly accurate and powerful, especially for such a small person. No offence Geoff."

"None taken," Geoff nodded.

"When I think back to that," Sion continued. "I'm amazed how they did it!"

"It's almost certainly who we think it is then," Geoff replied, looking for input from the others. "They'd do that, no problem. You see Sion, as Quinny may have mentioned, we cave dwellers are generally very good at self-defence. Martial arts you'd say, I suppose. That includes skills like throwing accuracy. That's Bijou, I'm certain of it."

"Bijou?" Sion was perplexed. "Who's Bijou?"

Chapter 27

How Could Bijou do it?

"A murderer, that's who." Geoff was once again beginning to weep as he recalled his late co-worker. He pulled a checked handkerchief from his trouser pocket. Wiping his eyes and blowing his nose like a foghorn, he continued. "We cave dwellers rarely argue or fight. We're gentle folk. Calm and collected. We resolve our problems or disagreements civilly. That's always been the way. Until *that* day. Over lunch, a group of us had been discussing which artefact we'd most like to own, if we could have any of them to keep. I said that I'd love to have the Faberge egg behind gate 1886. It's the most beautiful thing I've ever seen and I know Katla would love it! Anyway, the choices were really varied, you know, from gold encrusted jewellery to fossils and bones. Patrice had said that he'd love to own Joan of Arc's sword. His family had come from Rouen in France, so it meant a lot to him. Well, Bijou was having none of that, claiming that, 'My family found it, so my family keep it!' We'd only been messing about, we knew that we would never actually keep these things, it was just a chat, for goodness sake." Geoff's voice began to break and Tarquin took over.

"Well said Geoff. After that, Sion, Bijou was really unpleasant to poor Patrice. Just silly like, ignoring 'im, tellin' others that he'd said things he hadn't. You know, daft stuff. Then one mornin', Patrice was walkin' past gate 1792. He stopped to look, as you do. Lit the candle to have a better look. Bang. Someone pushes him into the gate, face first. He shouts, a few people look up, included Geoff here," Tarquin gestured towards Geoff, who was now sobbing into his saturated handkerchief. "That was that. Patrice was pushed from the ledge."

"So, do you definitely know it was Bijou?" Sion asked, even though he was certain of the answer.

"Definitely," Tarquin answered. "They'd had all these run-ins durin' the days before and then after the push, Bijou was not seen again. Gone. Of course, everyone who saw what 'appened was more concerned about poor Patrice than watchin' where the culprit went. Must've just scarpered."

"So when did all this happen? Was it very recently?"

"Nah. Terry, how many years d'you reckon now? Thirty, forty maybe?"

"It'll be nearly forty years," Terry confirmed without looking up from his teacup. "Before Quinny or I were 'ere."

"Goodness," Sion began. "So this Bijou will be how old now?"

Geoff looked up. He'd stopped crying and had given up with his drenched hankie. "It's hard to say, Sion. If they were still here, in the cave then it'd be similar to me, so one hundred and eighty six, but as they've absconded outside they'll almost certainly be claiming to be much younger. We live a long time, not forever, but for a good while longer than most people outside do. Probably because we've never been affected by illnesses and plagues. We are poorly sometimes, but nothing major. If they keep well and healthy, a cave dweller who's nearing two hundred years, like me, could easily live as a fifty year old."

"So what's the plan? Is there one?" Sion was eager. He so wanted to be a part of this. To help catch a criminal. Bring them to justice. Although, right now, he had no idea how he was going to be able to do much at all. He was at school five days a week. He wasn't always free at weekends and it was coming up to Christmas soon. He'd got a feeling they were staying away for a week of that.

"Right now Sion, we're trying to work out how Bijou might try to get back in," Geoff had now completely recovered from his previous tears. "As Quinny has told you, the vent near your school has gone. Filled in. We'll be sorting a new one nearby at some point, but not yet." Geoff paused while he munched his way through another biscuit. Sion did the same. "So the most likely thing is, they'll try to get through the vent by the sand dunes. It's a few miles north of the other one, a bit far for you to visit alone. So, the plan is that Terry will be staying there and watching it daily for any unusual goings on. Quinny will be working for a few weeks or so, a distance away, unfortunately." Tarquin bowed his head in disappointed agreement. "So your role is simple, Sion. Keep looking around for the figure you saw." Sion looked slightly downhearted at his seemingly humdrum task.

"But where? Back in the woods?"

"No! Do not go back there please!" Geoff's tone was firm. "Anywhere you go. It might sound boring, but believe me, if you saw Bijou again and let us know when and where, you could be saving not just the day, but our whole lives and the cave. It's massively important!" Sion was not convinced that his role was as crucial as Geoff was making out, but he agreed. Geoff held out a hand for Sion to shake, which he did. Firmly, to ensure that Geoff could feel his dedication.

"Come on Sion," Tarquin broke the silence. "We've had a good natter today. You need to be back?" Sion checked his watch.

"Yes, yes I do! I'll keep my eyes peeled and will let you know if I see anything." Sion got up to leave, shaking each gentleman's hand. Again, firmly. "I'll see you all soon. Keep me updated, won't you?"

"Certainly will m'boy," Tarquin agreed.

Chapter 28

Are We Festive Yet?

The following few weeks were uneventful, as far as Bijou related espionage was concerned. Christmas seemed to be everywhere, as usual. Sion was absolutely certain that Slade's 'Merry Christmas Everybody' was set to come on as he walked into any shop, or any room for that matter. Noddy Holder's screeching was making Sion cringe and did not make him feel remotely festive. Gwen had reverted to her usual December personality, which resembled a crazed fairy who'd swallowed a thousand blue Smarties with a litre of Lucozade. She kept trying to secretly tie tinsel to Sion or onto his clothing. She'd been successful once. He'd arrived at school one Thursday morning with a pink tinsel tail that'd been looped through his belt. Morgan had found it particularly amusing and had taken to calling Sion 'Pink Panther' for the rest of the day. After that, Sion had checked everything before leaving the house and again when arriving at school, just in case.

He'd not seen a single person that'd made him suspicious, which was beginning to infuriate him. He'd not heard from Tarquin at all, despite sending him several emails. He was beginning to think that he'd been pushed aside, given a job that was so pointless so that it'd keep him busy and away from the real work. He was downhearted and felt pessimistic about the whole affair. He'd even considered wandering down to the woods again, by the school, just on the off chance, but he'd chickened out. If anything did happen, he'd definitely be off the team, not that he was on it, or so he felt.

As he hadn't been back to Geoff's for a few weeks, Sion had started taking Albert on his walks again, much to Albert's delight. Gwen had persuaded their mother to buy a flashing Christmas collar, which Sion was not impressed by at all, but he'd been forbidden to remove it and accused of being a 'bah humbug', by all three family members. So, reluctantly, Sion was walking a Great Dane who was sporting a sporadically flashing Christmas tree for a collar.

School wasn't much better for Sion, as December moved on. Everyone was talking about Christmas. Some friends were going on holiday. Rhys' family were all going to the Caribbean for ten days. At least ten of Sion's classmates were hoping for the new X Box as a present. And then there was the school's production. A rendition of A Christmas Carol, but with lots of singing. Sion hadn't tried for a part, but he had been roped in, along with some other friends, to help with the sets. Their lessons in the last two weeks had nearly all been replaced by set building. The art teacher Mr Davies was jolly, not in a festive way, just jolly in general. He'd tell rude jokes and let them make themselves tea, if they brought him one too. He liked biscuits, a lot and would easily get through a packet of custard creams with one cup of tea. Hours spent with Mr Davies and a paint brush flew by. They'd all giggle as the music teacher lost her cool with a girl in Year 9, who would repeatedly sing the wrong verse. She was yet to get it right the first time. Then there was Lois, who was not quite able to reach the high note required, so opted for a noise similar to a cat in distress. Every time, Mr Davies would wince, "Oooo, dear!" As he grasped his ears.

The only downside to helping with the set, was that Mrs Anderson made a lot of the costumes. Despite her faults, you couldn't argue with her crafting skills. She'd made hats, jumpers, dresses, snowballs and many other bits and bobs. She'd actually been quite pleasant, maybe as she was in her element with her sewing kit, knitting and crocheting needles. There was the occasional bark at a disgruntled pupil, but she'd been friendly to Sion and his friends, even joined them and Mr Davies for cups of tea. On one of these tea breaks, she'd asked Sion how he'd been settling since moving from England.

"Fine thank you Mrs Anderson. I'm enjoying it now," He'd responded, hoping that was the end of the conversation.

"Where about are you living?" she continued.

Sion gave her a rough idea without divulging too much. He certainly did not want Mrs Anderson turning up for mince pies!

"Oh lovely, I bet you've got a good view from there. The hillside and the river. There's a cave near there isn't there? I've walked that way a few times."

Sion was startled by the question and thought for a moment before replying.

"Er, I think I remember seeing something like that."

Mrs Anderson smiled at him and continued to sip her tea.

The day of the production came. Even though Sion wasn't in it, his parents came to watch and brought Gwen with them. There wasn't a Christmas panto' on anywhere near them, so this was the closest thing. Sion's role was to change set panels and help James from Year 10 to get changed. He was playing Bob Cratchit, but also the Ghost of Christmas Present. He needed assistance to get into the festively decorated sumo suit for the latter role. The evening passed and that was that. Christmas in a few days and school over until the first week of January. Finally, Sion felt fleetingly festive. It'd been a high-spirited evening, everyone seemed chirpy, there was a buzz in the air. He forgot about Bijou, the cave, the sword and Patrice, just for a few hours, he forgot.

Chapter 29

How Can I Pass This Lull in Time?

The air was crisp and the garden frosty on the first day of Sion's Christmas holiday and he'd been left alone from half past eight. His father was still at work for two more days and his mother had taken Gwen Christmas shopping. They'd been dropped at the station and had gone on the train to Manchester. The offer had been made for Sion to go with them, but the thought of Christmas shopping with his tinsel-mad sister would've wiped any festive spirit Sion did have, out in an instant. He opted instead for a big bowl of Shreddies in front of the tv, in his pyjamas. After watching football match highlights and two episodes of Antiques Road Trip, Sion got dressed and retrieved Albert's lead from the back of the door. The almost inaudible jangling alerted Albert, who excitedly skidded around the tiled kitchen floor, occasionally crashing into the central table, while Sion put on his puffer jacket, gloves and beanie hat. Sion stood by the door to enjoy the stillness of the day. It was silent. The cold air stung his nose, but the fresh scent of winter felt calming. He decided not to walk towards the cave today, instead opting for a gentle stroll around the lanes, maybe finding a different footpath to explore, one without a stile preferably. For the first mile, Sion and Albert did not have to stand aside for a single vehicle. They came to a footpath sign in the hedge. It seemed to go around the other side of the hill where the cave was. Sion wondered if it joined up with the path outside the cave that he'd seen others walk around. He stood for a few moments to survey it. It was a stile of sorts, but was so low, Albert stepped over it with ease and began to bound up the path, taking full benefit of his extendable lead, awestruck sheep jumping away like the parting of woollen waves. This path was more forgiving than the one opposite Sion's house. It was a gentle climb to the top of the hill, slowly edging diagonally with the occasional zigzag. The view from this side was very different too. Facing the opposite direction almost, the hill now overlooked the sea in the distance. You could see more of the river and lots of wooded areas. Sion could see the town where his father was working right now and could make out the roof of his school. The feeling of cold had gone as Sion sat enjoying the view and the tranquillity. There were more sounds to be heard here, the hum of the main road, sheep, a tractor or bus, but you still felt far removed from any stresses. The pair sat for some time, just watching. Well, Albert was dozing, but still, he was relaxed and had no desire to bounce off anywhere. Sion had seen the bus go past his house, he'd then watched its journey towards the town, with only slight breaks in his sight of it, when the bus went behind trees. Eventually, it disappeared from view, probably only minutes away from its destination in town.

"Good morning Sion. Is this your dog?" Sion turned sharply, jarring his neck.

"Oh, hello Mrs Anderson. Off for a walk?" Sion rubbed at his neck. Mrs Anderson had a dog with her too, but its whole body was smaller than Albert's head alone. He sniffed at the visitor, the breath out from his nostrils made the diminutive dog's ears flap. "This your dog?" Sion asked. "This is Albert. He's a Great Dane."

"No, it's not my dog. I'm walking him for my neighbour. Not sure on the breed. He's called Ernie. Anyway, I'll be off now. I've been out longer than I planned." And with that, Mrs Anderson continued to hobble along the path, until she disappeared from view around the hill. Sion got up and began to walk in the opposite direction, towards the cave and ultimately back home. They walked leisurely, occasionally stopping for Sion to look at or listen to something. A chinook helicopter had startled both of them as it seemingly appeared from nowhere over the brim of the hill, Sion had heard the dim rumble in the distance, but it had still made him jump. Coming around the bend in the path, the cave suddenly came into view, quicker than Sion had thought it would. Sitting on the familiar stone outside was Terry. He was wearing the same coat and hat as he had on all the other meetings they'd had, but this time the feather was on the opposite side of his hat.

"Sion! Great to see you!" Terry boomed, before beginning to whisper. "Any sightin's?"

"Nothing, sorry. You heard from Tarquin? I've had no replies to my messages. Last time I heard from him was when we were all together at Geoff's."

"Not much, no. I know he's somewhere in Scotland doin' some work with the van, movin' stuff like. Probably not much signal. He said he'd be off for a bit over Christmas, so 'opefully, I'll 'ear more soon. What's the date now?"

"Twenty second," Sion replied, checking his watch from habit, even though he knew.

"Ok, so should 'ear soon. What you up to now, then?"

"Just going home. I've been walking Albert. You?"

"Going back to my little camp now. I've just had some lunch with Geoff and Katla. Fit to burst." Terry had been scratching Albert's head and the dog was now in a near-coma state, head settled on Terry's knee and drool dripping from his sagging chops.

"Well, hopefully catch up soon. Do tell Tarquin to message, if you see or hear from him. Hope you have more luck than me."

"See y'lad. Bye pooch!" Terry saluted as the pair began their descent. Sion did not look back until he reached the door, by which time Terry was nowhere to be seen.

As Sion was fending for himself today, his lunch consisted of two potato waffles (cooked in the toaster) and microwaved baked beans. He completed his haute cuisine feast with two mini Snickers bars that he found in the fridge and a can of Fanta. The afternoon was spent lying on the sofa watching Santa Claus the Movie and Countdown. Sion had thoroughly enjoyed his day to himself, he appreciated his own company and Albert's. Tyres on gravel. The serenity was about to be broken. Albert acknowledged it too and began to bark and leap at the window. Sion called him back in the hope that he hadn't showered the window panes in drool again. Gwen had hurried inside, laden with bags and ran straight upstairs.

"Sion! Where are you?"

"In the lounge with Albert."

"He'd best not be on the sofa or eating chocolate biscuits!"

"No, he's fine," Sion lied, pushing a disgruntled Albert onto the floor and brushing any visible fur off. He got up and went to greet his parents.

"What have you done with yourself today then, Sion?" his father asked.

"Well, I took Albert out for a good walk for a few hours and watched a film. Not much."

"You eaten?"

"Just Shreddies this morning and some waffles and beans for lunch. What's for dinner, I'm starving?"

"Stir fry with noodles. That ok?"

"Yeah, I need some veg'. Good time shopping?"

"Yes, thank you. Gwen spent most of her money on herself though and chose the most expensive meal from the menu at lunch time! Wish we'd never introduced her to seafood!"

As his parents returned to their chat, Sion moseyed up to his room and opened up his laptop. An email! He'd finally got a reply from Tarquin.

Hi Sion,

Sorry I've missed your messages, I've been so busy and not always had signal or wifi. Finished now though and will be on my way home later. Just a quick message, to keep your eyes open, as Terry has seen Bijou, we think. Well someone was doing something near the dunes when he got back there today and someone has been in his tent. Could be kids, no offence, but we need to be mindful of the possibilities.

He said he'd seen you today.

Anyway, will message again when I get back.

Quinny

Much to Sion's annoyance, while he was forced to spend the next few days visiting family and friends, with Gwen and his parents, Tarquin and Terry kept watch at the dunes. The vent in question was an unusual one as it was concealed under a large rock on a small peninsula of land that was cut off by the tide, twice a day. This was impinging on Bijou's progress, it would seem. The vent itself was rarely affected by the water, but getting close enough to it for an extended period, without being soaked by waves was challenging. Tarquin and Terry, despite the seriousness of their work, had to suppress giggles when Bijou was knocked over, face planting the floor, by one such wave. By dinner time on Christmas Eve, Tarquin had left Terry to pack up the last of his things. Both men were going to have a Christmas dinner the following day with Geoff and Katla. From what they'd witnessed, no one would be able to do anything significant at the vent, unless they'd acquired an ability to shrink to the size of a mouse.

Chapter 30

Whose Fireworks on the Hill?

Merry Christmas Sion!

Presume you're still at home. If so, make sure you're looking up at the cave at seven o'clock sharp, tonight. You'll see why.

Nothing else to report. Let me know if you manage to see.

Have a good one,

Quinny.

It was Christmas morning. Sion was the first up. Gwen always made a great deal of noise when she surfaced on Christmas Day, so she must still be sleeping. It was only 5 am after all. Sion had been awake for over an hour and had been perched on his window seat with his laptop, ever since. He couldn't imagine what was going to happen at seven o'clock that evening, but he was resolute that whatever it was, it wasn't going to be missed. He set an alarm on his mobile for ten minutes to seven, just in case he was too busy or distracted. Surely it couldn't be anything too ridiculous. Other people might see.

"Enough!" Sion told himself, as he slammed his laptop shut. His tummy was rumbling and he really wanted a cup of tea, although he didn't want to wake Gwen. He loved the peace in the morning before others woke up, it felt like his own secret time of the day. Gwen's door was ajar as Sion passed it. He glanced inside. She was still asleep, one foot hanging out from under her garishly pink duvet. He slinked down the stairs, trying to keep to the right, as it didn't creak as much and missing out the step, two from the bottom. In the kitchen, Albert was snoring loudly in his basket. He opened an eye, looked at Sion briefly, before returning to his comatose state with a long, drawn-out grunt. Sion sat down at the kitchen table with his tea and toast, which was predictably slathered in Marmite. He'd almost forgotten that it was Christmas Day. He'd not opened anything, apart from the email, the fridge, a milk bottle and the Marmite jar and was perfectly content just sitting alone in the almost silent kitchen, lit only by the moon and a plug-in nightlight. As the last bit of toast went into his mouth, Sion heard Gwen squealing excitedly from upstairs. He refilled the kettle and prepared a teapot for everyone. By the time he entered his parents' room with the tray, Gwen had opened her whole stocking, wrapping paper strewn across the polished floor boards. Gwen gathered up her stocking fillers and returned elatedly to her room. Within seconds, music was blaring, clearly a new CD had been among the gifts. Sion took his time unwrapping his stocking presents, examining each carefully and sipping at his second mug of tea, while his parents sat in bed, still not quite awake.

Christmas Day in Sion's house was not usually a busy affair and this year was no exception to that tradition. Sion's mother had once again opted for a duck for dinner, owing to her hatred of turkey. Just a few friends around later in the day and then off to visit family in England on the 27th of December, or 'Christmas Two', as Gwen had been calling it. Aside from his thoughts about that night's 'event', Sion was still eager to find out what he'd had for Christmas. He'd not thought to ask for anything specific this year, his mind had been on other things.

"You're too old for stockings now, Sion. Don't you think so?" Sion's father suggested.

"No!" came the rather abrupt reply.

Sion was perfectly happy with the idea of getting a stocking on Christmas morning for as long as he lived with his parents and then if they wanted to keep the magic alive, one could be delivered to him in his own house, after that. It seemed like a great idea to him and he was sure that on this, Gwen would agree with him.

Sion had added another pile of discarded paper to the floor boards. He'd had some water bombs, miscellaneous sweets, a selection of miniature chocolates, a paper plane kit and the ubiquitous mug and Christmas themed socks. He always had a new mug. Which was good, as he was prone to smashing them. This one changed colour when warm liquid was added, revealing an image of the Liverpool FC logo.

"It's amazing how Santa knows which team I support!" Sion whispered to his father, with a wink.

Sion and Gwen usually waited until after their Christmas lunch for their main presents. As a younger child, it had been torture, but Sion wasn't bothered by it now, especially as their mother liked to eat at actual lunch time and not midway through the afternoon.

It had been worth the wait this year. Sion's present couldn't have been more perfect. A drone, his very own drone. He couldn't wait to use it! Predictably, his father wanted to read the instruction manual cover to cover prior to its first outing. Sion was slightly suspicious that this present had actually been chosen by his father for his own enjoyment! Some family gifts kept Sion amused for a time, while he waited for his father to prepare the drone for its test flight. He'd had a football facts book and a history encyclopaedia. He thumbed through this and stopped on a double page spread about Joan of Arc. He read it twice, from beginning to end, no mention of the elusive sword.

Albert had had a new toy with the most ear-splitting squeak. Everyone winced at every chew. Had it not been the reason for his father suddenly being ready to go out with the drone, Sion would've stripped the dog of his beloved new toy. It was a tremendously unpleasant noise.

Sion and his father sent the drone into the sky above their house, narrowly avoiding the ancient sycamore tree by the gravel drive. It whirred through the air and was surprisingly easy to control. Sion's father explained that it would take videos, which could then be cut into single pictures on his laptop. It was hands down, the best Christmas present Sion had ever had and it may end up being a very useful one.

As the drone was expertly landed onto the grass in front of the house, the sound of chattering people came into earshot. His mother's friends had arrived and they'd clearly been making merry already. One lady swayed slightly as she handed Sion's father a bottle of something. She'd also attempted to kiss him on the cheek, but had missed and got his ear instead. Sion collected the drone and followed the others inside, checking his watch. Just under three hours until the surprise. He checked his mobile phone, to make sure the alarm was still set. He decided to temporarily hibernate upstairs, the guests were loud and were already taking Snapchat selfies, including several with poor Albert, who was being treated like a canine celebrity.

Sion let the time tick by and the guests pickle themselves downstairs. He sat in his usual spot, in the window, laptop perched on knee, occasionally gazing through the glass, as the view in front of him became darker and darker.

His chiming alarm woke him. He'd nodded off, head against the window pane. He yelped slightly as he flexed the crick in his neck, before sliding off the seat and grabbing his hoodie. As he went outside his father appeared.

"What you doing? It's a bit late for the drone."

"Oh. I thought I saw something from the hill. Just going to look from outside." To Sion's dismay, his father followed him out. He was undoubtedly trying to make his escape from the gaggle of tipsy ladies, who were still shrieking from the lounge.

The two of them gazed up at the hill, Sion's eyes fixed on where he knew the cave opening was. He glanced at his watch. 18:59.

"Look!" Sion's father pointed up as a glowing light appeared on the hillside. "Maybe someone has fireworks."

Whoosh! A fiery, amber rocket shot into the sky and exploded into a giant symbol. Sion knew exactly what it was, his father did not. Within seconds it had vanished into the night sky.

"Freemasons I reckon," Sion's dad remarked as he turned to go in. "They like their symbols."

Sion wasn't sure what his father was talking about, but he was sure Google would know. He'd check later. First job was to let Tarquin know that he'd seen. He smiled as he closed the door. This had been a great Christmas Day, but right now, Sion was ready for some sleep.

Chapter 31

What to expect?

As per schedule, the Christmas holidays vanished in a flash. Before Sion knew it, it was the beginning of a new year and only a few days until Sion and Gwen returned to school. Sion had not received a single correspondence from Tarquin, since the firework on Christmas Day. To be fair, Sion hadn't messaged either. So two days before the new term, Sion emailed Tarquin, with the hope of an update on the Bijou situation, but also as a distraction from his homework, which as usual, he'd left longer than he should've.

Tarquin's reply came within the hour. It was brief and slightly disappointing. Bijou had not been seen since before Christmas and they didn't know where she was. That was it. Sion sighed, closed his laptop and returned to his copy of Great Expectations, which he had to finish before the following Tuesday. He was becoming quite fond of the character, Pip, and had to admit, it was a great story. At least, he was glad he'd chosen this one, instead of Wuthering Heights, which hadn't appealed to him at all.

By the time his mother called him for their evening meal, Sion was coming to the end of the final chapter. He'd been completely absorbed by the story and took a moment or two to return his mind to real life and establish the reason for his name being called.

Sion remained in a post-book state of zombification, for the remainder of the evening. Responding to questions with grunts, while reliving aspects of Dickens' world in his mind, over and over. As he contemplated the actions of Abel once more, Sion thought of Tarquin. For reasons unknown, even to himself, he had used Tarquin as an image for Abel, while reading. Sion reflected on his emailed reply. Why had Bijou just gone from the radar? Where had she gone? Maybe she had been celebrating Christmas with family and friends, if she had any? Tomorrow was Sion's final full day at home, before the new school term. A wander up to Geoff's was in order. First thing tomorrow. No matter what the weather.

Chapter 32

Could it be Her?

Getting up before dawn, after a few weeks without an alarm, was good practice for the next day. With everyone still, presumably asleep in bed and Albert flat out, half in and half out of his basket, Sion silently left his home behind and began to trudge across the field, towards the steep path. The ground beneath his feet was soggy and as the elevation increased, Sion's feet slipped frequently, slowing his progress. By the time he neared flatter ground, he was using his hands as support, to prevent himself from making a rapid descent. Picking the mud from his nails, Sion got to his feet and surveyed the view of home and the surrounding hills. He found the lack of sound almost deafening at times, but pleasant. Buzzards circling overhead, made the occasional cry, sheep from countless distances, called to one another and water flowed at varying speeds. There was always a sound of water coming from somewhere. Be it a drip or a flurry. It was one of the best parts about living there, in Sion's opinion.

He glanced at his watch. It was still very early. Maybe too early to just drop in on Geoff and Katla. Sion pulled a cereal bar from his pocket and wandered past the cave and around the corner to a large stone, which he'd perched on previously. Hours could pass, while you sat there, gazing across the valley to the sea and the town. There was always something to watch, be it physical, man-made, wild or human. Sion checked his pockets for the binoculars that he knew weren't going to be there and cursed to himself. The bell of a church in the town, chimed to confirm seven o'clock. Thirty minutes, Sion thought. Thirty minutes, then he'd make his way to Geoff's. He continued to gaze out towards the sea, where he could just make out a large fishing trawler, as it chugged out of the fog, leaving a shimmering wake behind it. Flickering specks around its stern, suggested a flock of ravenous seagulls trying to scavenge what they could.

The sound of feet and breathlessness startled him. A short, cloaked person was shuffling along the path, towards his seat. They had not yet noticed him, as their head repeatedly turned to examine the path behind them. The hood was removed and the head turned forward. Eyes locked to each other in momentary stillness. Mrs Anderson was standing in front of Sion. She was panting and appeared to be wet.

"Goodness, Sion! Have you seen my dog?" Her breath wheezy and words slightly slurred. She was clearly in a state of panic.

"The one you were walking when I saw you here before?" Sion replied.

"Yes! Yes, that one! Have you seen it?" A sharp intake of breath. "No? Ok, I'd better go." Sion stood and watched her, scuttling along the path and out of sight. Random things had happened to him before, but this was probably the most outlandish. If he remembered correctly, the dog she'd been walking before, hadn't been hers. Sion acknowledged to himself that you would be fairly panicked if you'd lost someone else's dog. As he began to walk towards the cave, he whistled a few times and looked around the valley for any sign of a loose dog. Nothing. Although, there was another noise. Sion whistled again.

"Help! Is someone there?"

Sion ran into the cave. From inside The Drop, he could hear splashing and gasping. He shone his torch into the hole.

"Who's there? That you, Quinny?"

"No, it's Sion."

"Oh, thank goodness. It's me, Terry. Shine it on't side, I can't find the way out. Me fingers are froz'n."

After a few minutes, a saturated and shivering Terry hauled himself onto the cave floor and panted momentarily on all fours, before getting to his feet. Without a word to Sion, who was temporarily rendered speechless, Terry pushed on the door. Nothing. Still panting for air, he gestured wildly to Sion, seemingly towards two stones on the other side of The Drop, where Sion was still standing, torch in hand. He understood and immediately followed the gesticulated instruction, before nimbly making his own way over to Terry, who was already half way through the doorway. The ear-splitting alarm began to penetrate Sion's ears and he pulled his hoodie top tight, in a pointless attempt to muffle the sound. Inside the cave, Terry was already in Geoff and Katla's house. Sion ran the stone steps and into a truly chaotic scene. Maurice was on his knees behind the armchair, Sion couldn't see why. Terry was now in agitated conversation with several other cave dwellers. Much of Geoff and Katla's living room furniture was upturned. Smashed ornaments, a spilled vase of flowers. And where were Geoff and Katla? Sion took a few steps closer to Maurice and his question was answered. There they were. Tied together, back to back on the rug. Geoff had a trickle of blood coming from one nostril and Katla was sniffling, tears making their way down her porcelain cheeks. They were both still in their nightwear, by the looks of it and Katla's hair was tied in an unkempt topknot. The alarm stopped. Sion removed his hoodie.

"She got it, Sion. She got it. I tried." Geoff was now crying quietly with his head down on his knees, as Maurice untied the frayed rope from around his and his wife's feet.

"Who? Got what?" As the questions left Sion's lips, a multitude of thoughts shot through his mind, like a meteor shower. "Bijou? The sword?" With what he thought must've been an audible 'thump', Sion made the chilling connection. He shuddered and stammered slightly, before finally managing to speak. "I saw her." Sion gulped and swallowed hard.

"You saw her? Where? Just now?" Geoff was on his feet, wiping the trail of blood onto his pyjama sleeve.

"Before I heard Terry shouting. And Geoff. I know her. She's called Mrs Anderson. She's a teacher at my school." Sion thought for a moment. Could he be wrong? Maybe she really was looking for a dog. Maybe she had nothing to do with it. Maybe he was adding two and two together to make a million.

"What?!" Geoff's shout alerted the others to Sion's potential disclosure and within moments, a circle had formed around the mat, where Katla still sat, sobbing gently into a handkerchief.

"What is it Geoff? What's going on?" Terry spoke first. All eyes followed Geoff's and scrutinised Sion, beckoning more information.

"I came to see you. It was early, so I waited on a rock, just down from the cave entrance. A lady suddenly appeared, from around the corner. She was hooded and wet. When she saw me, I recognised her. She's my RE teacher, Mrs Anderson." Sion paused. He was very aware of his short, brief sentences. "She told me she was looking for a dog and asked if I'd seen it. I hadn't, so she ran off down the path. She was wet, which I did think was strange. Anyway," Sion continued, "I came to the cave entrance and I could hear shouting. It was Terry." Terry nodded in agreement.

"What's RE?" called a voice from the back, which was ignored due to its irrelevance.

"Did she have anything in her hands?" one of the other cave dwellers asked.

"Not that I could see. But she had a big overcoat, like a cloak, on. So maybe, she could've had something concealed. I really don't know."

"It must be her. It must be Bijou!" Maurice added. His voice trembled slightly.

"I just can't believe it!" Sion blurted out. All eyes turned to him, once more. "I mean, she's my teacher! She's been at the school for ages and lots of people know her. How could she be Bijou? Wouldn't someone know?"

"Who? It's not like we're famous, Sion," Geoff replied, now more softly. "If she chose to disappear into the world, all those years ago, what better way to do it, than be a teacher. She wouldn't be obviously different and she'd have an identity. Now Sion, can you think of anything about her, which might now give us any clues? Anything that's happened in the past."

Sion thought. Actually, there was something. Two things in fact. "Well, she had a broken foot for a while and it was around the time of the breach in the woods and also, I've seen her up here once before. Walking the dog she said she was looking for today."

"Well gentlemen, and Katla," Geoff continued, "I think we've got her. Now, we need to think very carefully about what to do next and how to do it."

"I'll put the kettle on, shall I?" Katla said, rising to her feet. She wiped away her tears and walked towards the kitchen, pushing smashed pottery to the side with her feet, as she went.

Chapter 33

Do I Know Her or Not?

By six the following morning, Sion had already dressed for school, read and replied to an email from Tarquin and prepared his bag. He was anxious, but eager to return. Would Mrs Anderson be there? Would she acknowledge their meeting on the hill? Would there be any clues regarding her alter ego? Sion's friends and classmates wouldn't have the first clue about anything out of the ordinary and it wasn't going to be easy, keeping it all from them. Especially with 'part one' of the plan being implemented after school. Sion had to admit, he was a little apprehensive about it all, but he trusted Tarquin.

Sion didn't need to wait until RE to find out if Mrs Anderson was in school. She was arriving into the school car park, as Sion's mum dropped him in the adjacent layby. She heaved a large jute bag from the back seat of her three-door hatchback and made her way in through the staff entrance, without even a glance towards Sion, who'd, in contrast, watched her every move.

As she bustled past her students and into the classroom, after lunch, Mrs Anderson looked Sion directly in the eye.

"Found him. Little rascal. He was by the car when I got down the hill."

"Oh. Good," Sion stammered. Rhys looked at him with complete bemusement. Sion decided that it'd be ok to divulge the meeting, so began to briefly explain the 'lost dog' situation, as they found their seats.

Had Sion not been party to the events of yesterday, he'd not have known that there was anything going on at all. Mrs Anderson was slightly buoyant, but nothing too over the top. The lesson was dull and they had to work in silence. He was, however, even more uneasy about the plan for after school and the time for action was fast approaching. Before he knew it, Tarquin's van was waiting in the layby. Sion sniggered through the classroom window, as he noticed Tarquin was 'reading' what Sion knew as a 'top shelfer' or 'toilet literature'. The school bell rang and the noise of moving chairs was quickly replaced by charging feet and loud voices. Outside, the loaded school buses began to roar away and parents pulled in and out of the layby. Sion crossed the road and climbed into Tarquin's van. His 'literature' had been hidden away, presumably under the driver's seat.

"Ready? Which car is it?" Tarquin craned his neck to see the staff car park.

"The small black one, by the door," Sion replied quietly and without pointing.

After less than ten minutes, Mrs Anderson appeared. She was not carrying her large bag and was very quickly pulling out of the car park.

"There. Now!" Sion shouted to Tarquin, who was straightening his bushy eyebrows in the rear view mirror.

Tarquin had thankfully left the engine running, so managed to get onto the road with just one car in-between them and Mrs Anderson's compact, Japanese hatchback. Sion had absolutely no idea where she lived or where she'd be going now. He had wondered what they'd do if she went to

Tesco for a 'big shop'. Surely, he couldn't be waiting all night with Tarquin. He needed to be home by six o'clock.

With one short stop at a Sainsbury's Local, they located Mrs Anderson's house within less than thirty minutes. She lived on the edge of a cul-de-sac, in the middle of a large estate, mainly comprising 1960s bungalows. All very similar in appearance, with the front door alternatively on the left or the right. There was almost always a small tree in the front garden and each bungalow had a drive and a garage with a painted metal door. Some had been modernised and/or extended, but Mrs Anderson's, number 63, looked like it had been the same since it had been built. It didn't seem to have double-glazed windows or even a modern door. The garden did have a tree, but was quite overgrown with shrubs and bindweed.

Tarquin parked the van away from number 63, but in view of the drive and front window. They saw the light go on and a figure walk towards the window and close the curtains. It was beginning to go dark outside. Sion yawned.

"What now?"

"Well, we know where to go now. So we'll report back and then plan 'part two'. Shall I drop you home?"

"Yes please," Sion replied wearily.

He needn't have worried about 'part one', it was a breeze. But not knowing anything about 'part two', was making Sion a bit nervous. He wasn't even sure if he was playing a part and if so, what it was. He'd have to just wait and see.

Chapter 34

What Will They Find?

Over the next few weeks, despite being in fairly regular correspondence with Tarquin, Sion had been feeling isolated. Tarquin's emails had been vague and limited in content. He longed to know what would happen next and how he was going to help bring Bijou to justice. Knowing that his RE teacher was actually a murderer and a thief, was quite a secret to keep while you sat in the classroom with your seemingly oblivious friends. It had even been hard calling her Mrs Anderson in class, now he was so certain of her real identity.

He'd had plenty of time to think about the unfolding story before him. Sion wondered what Patrice had been like and if he'd been as hospitable a person as his friend, Geoff. He didn't know much really, at all, about these amazing people or their vast hordes of treasure. The visit to the larger cave had blown his mind, but that was just the start. He knew that there were thousands of objects, hidden away underground, throughout the warren of caves and tunnels. Maybe Sion could offer to log all of the treasures on a spreadsheet for them, he was good at that. He'd be able to find out what was there for himself and help the cave dwellers out at the same time. It was going to have to wait though, there were more pressing issues ahead.

The email Sion had been waiting for, came on a Thursday, just after 9pm. It was brief, but clear. Sion would need an excuse to be out the following evening, maybe a gathering with friends in town or a cinema trip would be sufficient. He'd done similar before, so it'd be nothing out of the ordinary. As suggested in the email, Sion packed a change of clothes into his school bag. The plan shouldn't be undertaken in his uniform. He also needed his mobile phone, gloves and as much courage as he could muster. To say that Sion now felt his role important, was an understatement.

Since their last meeting, Tarquin had been gathering information about Bijou's daily routine that'd help with the plan. He'd found out that, apart from school, she leaves the home every week on a Friday at around 6pm, as she is a member of a ten-pin bowling group. She is usually home at just after 7.30pm. Tarquin confirmed that he'd never once seen anyone else go into her bungalow, although, like several other residents of the estate, she does have a mobile fishmonger, who visits on a Monday evening. While watching her movements, Tarquin had also deduced that the garage door, despite not being used as a garage, was always unlocked and that there was an internal door to the house inside. This, he suggested, would be their way in, to avoid any breaking and entering. Sion was very grateful for this. Playing a role in her downfall was one thing, but a criminal record was not on his agenda.

So that was that. As the pupils filed out of school on Friday afternoon, Sion clambered, once again, into Tarquin's van. They'd have a bit of a wait until Bijou had left for bowling, so they visited the McDonald's 'drive through' in town and sat to eat in the carpark, watching a family of resident rats and discussing the plan and possible problems they might encounter. If she didn't leave as expected then the plan would be postponed. If the garage door was locked, the same. Sion was most concerned about being in the bungalow when she returned. Tarquin was not going in with him, as he'd be waiting in the van, around the corner. He reminded Sion to keep his mobile phone at hand, but on silent.

They drove onto the estate at 5.45pm and parked four bungalows down from Bijou's. The onset of spring meant it was still light, but a fine, misty drizzle made visibility poor. Sion checked his watch again. 5.57pm. Headlights beamed from the driveway of number sixty-three and Bijou's car pulled out slowly, turning left up the hill and out of the estate. As to not alert neighbours, Tarquin resisted turning his engine back on for a few minutes. Sion checked the time once more. 6.03pm.The van eased forward and the handbrake creaked. In the back, Tarquin had brought a large sealed cardboard box. They would carry the box to the garage, open the hopefully unlocked door and place the box inside, like a delivery to a safe place. Sion would then nip into the house through the internal door, which they also hoped was unlocked, while Tarquin went back to the van and drove to the next street.

The box was heavy and awkward, not helped by the height difference between Sion and Tarquin.

"What've you put in here?" Sion whispered across the box to Tarquin.

"A bag of compost," came the response. "A big one."

They set it down in front of the garage door and Tarquin tried the handle. It was stiff and was not keen to budge. After a few nervous wiggles, a click and a gentle shove, the door began to lift above their heads. As planned, Sion reversed into the garage with Tarquin facing in, directing him with the box. A space on top of an old under-unit fridge was perfect.

"Good luck, Sion. Just do your best and message, when yer need me. Yer feelin' ok?"

Sion nodded, pulling his phone from his pocket and turning on the torch. He tried the internal door. To his relief it was unlocked, as they'd suspected. Anxiety rushed through Sion, as he knew he'd have to begin the next phase of the task.

Tarquin turned, walked out of the garage and closed the metal door with a bang.

Chapter 35

Will I Survive This Mission?

Very aware of the limited time and the need to leave the bungalow undisturbed, Sion began scanning around the first room, keeping his torch low, as to not alert anyone to his presence. The door from the garage opened into a hallway. The carpet had thick pile, which squashed beneath his feet. Before moving further, he flicked away the dirt that he'd trodden in on his trainers. From the hallway, Sion could see five internal doors, all closed and the front door. He tried the first. This was a bedroom. Quite empty, apart from a single bed, fitted wardrobe and a bookshelf. Sion got down to his knees and attempted to shine the torch under the bed. It was a divan. Nothing there, but one large drawer by Sion's knees. He pulled it gently open. Empty. Returning to his feet, Sion left the room, quietly closing the door behind him.

The second door, led into the bathroom. Again, small and basic. Nowhere obvious to hide a large sword. Once again, Sion closed the door carefully.

Third door. Another bedroom. This time larger with a double bed, a clothes rail and more books. As the torch shone over the clothes, Sion recognised a few items from Mrs Anderson's limited wardrobe of colours. Lots of browns and pastels. Again, on his knees, Sion scrutinised the space under the bed. This one was not a divan, but had very little underneath it. Just some shoes, some crutches and an ancient, rusting ironing board.

Sion concealed his torch, as he passed the front door and tried the next handle on the corridor. This was the kitchen. As Sion had anticipated, it was dated. Brown and beige MDF units and cupboards, with two wooden stools pushed under a 'breakfast bar'. It was clean and tidy, with a faint smell of recently grilled sausages. Each cupboard was opened and almost immediately closed. It'd never fit into any of them. He checked under the units and with the collection of mops and brushes, behind the door. The sudden glow and roar of the gas boiler, above his head, made Sion jump and gasp. He checked his phone. No news from Tarquin was good.

6.32 pm.

There was one door left on the corridor, which Sion presumed was a living room. It was at the front of the house. It was the room they'd seen Bijou closing the curtains in. He'd have to turn the torch off for now. Opening the door, slowly, Sion crawled in, on his hands and knees. He couldn't remember the height of the window and if it looked directly at the bungalow opposite.

"Woah!" Sion exclaimed, as he scooted across the carpet, towards an old sewing table, in the opposite corner.

Lying across the table, uncovered, for all to see, was the sword. Sion gulped and wiped his now sweaty palms onto his jeans. Fingers trembling, he messaged Tarquin. Simply writing, 'found it'.

Sion reached for the sword with both hands. He trembled as he lowered it and himself to the carpet. It was a substantial weight. It looked and felt and smelt like Bijou had been polishing or cleaning it. His mobile phone vibrated and startled him once more. 'Get to the garage, now', came the brief reply. Sion 'walked' back towards the living room door, on his knees, pulling the sword alongside. Once through the door, he got to his feet and made haste to the garage. His phone began to vibrate in his pocket. It didn't stop. Someone was calling him. Sion ignored it and stepped into the garage. As he pulled the door closed behind him, his phone began to vibrate again and as it did, Sion looked up to see the garage door being illuminated by headlights, presumably Tarquin's.

Sion took his phone from his pocket. Three missed calls from Tarquin. As Sion pressed redial, all became apparent. It wasn't Tarquin's headlights. It was Bijou's!

Panic set in. Cancelling the call, Sion frantically scoured the garage for a hiding place. Anywhere he could cower and conceal himself and the sword. He wondered if he'd use it in self-defence, if it came to it. He wasn't feeling very brave, especially as he knew Bijou had killed one of the last people who'd got in her way. Sion found a large, garden waste sack. He sat crossed-legged at the back of the garage, behind a large black dustbin, sword pointing upright, between his knees and pulled the sack carefully over his head, hiding his shoes. He waited in silence. He'd not yet heard the car door open and close, although, he might just not have noticed in his panicked state. He fumbled for his phone. Tarquin had now rung six times and had sent two messages. One to say that Bijou was turning into the drive and one to tell Sion to hide. Quickly, Sion messaged back to confirm his hiding place. He returned his phone to his pocket and waited.

At least ten seconds passed, before the car door opened outside the garage and almost immediately closed. Sion heard the faint noises of Bijou, as she walked towards the front door and put the key into the lock. Light came into the garage from under the internal door, Sion could make out the line, through the hessian sack. He sat, once again being deafened by the silence. Every now and again, he'd hear a sound from the bungalow and he imagined what he thought she was doing. He wondered how long it'd be before she noticed. What would she do? You couldn't call the police to report an item stolen that you'd stolen yourself, surely. Try to matter-of-factly explain to a Police Officer that you'd got Joan of Arc's missing sword and that someone had taken it from you.

He continued to sit in silence. His legs becoming numb and his bottom cold from the concrete floor. He was certain that there was a spider in the sack, as something kept touching his forehead, but this was not the time to panic about a spider. A raging murderer was a more terrifying prospect, so Sion sat tight, ignoring the arachnid's sporadic strokes and his own aching legs.

His phone vibrated. Sion tried to reach it without disturbing the sack. It was Tarquin, again. Apparently, the living room light had not gone on yet. Bijou would not yet know about her missing sword. She must be busy, maybe preparing food or changing. At the exact moment that his phone vibrated again, Sion heard a scream from the bungalow. Bijou was repeatedly shouting 'no', in panicked shrieks. Sion could hear stamping feet and doors being slammed erratically.

Silence.

Sion jumped as the garage's internal door swung open, slamming into the old fridge, pushing Tarquin's box onto the floor with a crash. The strip light flickered momentarily before illuminating the garage. Sion had no idea if he could be seen through the sack and was finding it increasingly difficult to sit still. He shivered with cold, fear and discomfort. Bijou had paused, maybe to examine the unfamiliar box that had fallen onto the ground, on her frantic entrance.

Sion closed his eyes in an attempt to control his breathing, but opened them hastily, when the main garage door crashed open, bringing with it a rush of cool air. Bijou's steps could be heard running from the garage and into the garden. She knew she couldn't alert anyone for help. Sion knew that too. What he didn't know was what she'd do next.

With her currently out of the garage, Sion messaged Tarquin to confirm that he was still hiding. A reply came instantly. A thumbs up emoji and 'Don't move, I'll keep you posted'.

Sion couldn't hear a sound from Bijou. He wasn't sure if she was back inside or still outside. His knees were throbbing now and a nervous sweat was trickling down his forehead. He must have been inside the sack for nearly twenty minutes.

Outside, a car door opened and shut. An engine started. Bijou's car was driving away. Its wheels spun, as it left the drive at speed. Sion turned his phone in his hand to see the screen, desperate for Tarquin to confirm her exit from the scene. It rang. Tarquin was calling.

"Sion, get out now! Quick as you can. I'm three doors up, by the junction."

He didn't need telling twice. Sion uncovered himself and tried to stand, wrapping the sword in the sack. His legs were like jelly, he stumbled, hunched over, as briskly as he could, from the garage like a drunk trying to catch the last bus home. The sword was cumbersome and slowed his pace further. By the time he got to the van, Sion felt like he'd reached the finishing line of a marathon. The relief and exhaustion made him dizzy and unable to even do his seatbelt, without Tarquin's assistance. With the weight of the wrapped sword on his already worn out legs, Sion leant back to regain his breath and composure, as Tarquin drove out of the estate and into the night.

Chapter 36

Is it in Safe Hands?

As much as he'd have liked to have been there, for the sword's return to the security of the cave, Sion was relieved to flop exhaustedly onto his bed. Still fully clothed and with his coat on, he was asleep within minutes, flat out until a cramp in his right leg woke him at twenty minutes to four in the morning. After clumsily de-coating himself and stumbling around his room for some jogging bottoms, Sion reassumed his place in the bed, pulling his duvet up close to his chin. This time he was not asleep instantly, nor was he close to it. His mind filled with snapshots of the previous night's escapade. His knees automatically rose up, creating a foetal position, when he thought of his time at the back of the garage. His breathing quickened as he imagined being there right now, beyond grateful to actually be safe in his bed. How had he done it? Was he a thief? Presumably, he technically was, but with good reason. As he began to drift in and out of consciousness, he thought of being arrested and sentenced. Mrs Anderson glaring at him from across a blurry courtroom. "Aaarrgghh!" Sion woke suddenly as Mrs Anderson came face to face with him, her breath on his nose, a scent of stale coffee.

Alarmed and slightly sweaty, Sion abandoned the plan of continued sleep, instead opting to tiptoe delicately down the stairs for a cup of tea and some toast. A recorded episode of Line of Duty, a hot drink, salty Marmite and the warmth of Albert on his feet, lulled him back into a sense of security. Although, after twenty minutes, the weight of the Great Dane was giving Sion cramp again. A displeased Albert padded off to his basket in the kitchen and Sion replaced him with a cushion. By the time the credits rolled, Sion was flat out, sleeping soundly, with his head draped over the arm of the chair. Not even a flinch when the rest of his family began their morning routine. To prevent Gwen from waking him, Sion's mother softly pulled the door and instructed his sister to leave him to sleep.

"Bless him, he must have had a bad dream and come downstairs. Leave him be please Gwen, you'll have to entertain yourself upstairs for now."

Gwen protested the aberration and her 'right' to watch TV on a Saturday, but her arguments landed on deaf ears. A stern point towards the stairs to appease and off she went, fractiously muttering to herself about being poorly treated and of Sion being their favourite.

It wasn't until nearly midday that Sion re-surfaced, with only a modicum of recollection of his early hours' snack. After clumsily rolling from the sofa, he staggered about for a time, wondering what his name was and where he lived. A bona fide, post-nap stupor. Once he'd established his credentials; that it was in fact a Saturday and he didn't need to go to school, he felt more able to dress himself and plan his day. It was while ferreting about in his top drawer for pants that Sion reflected on the previous evening. Presumably, the sword was safely back 'home' now; goodness knows where Bijou had got to. A visit to Geoff was in order. Right after he'd located his left trainer, which he'd obviously, carelessly flung somewhere last night.

When finally on his way up the hill, Sion thought about how he'd like to take Albert to meet everyone. Maybe there'd be a way of getting him across The Drop. Or maybe not. He'd definitely ask though. Albert would surely be an instant celebrity in the caves.

After saying his 'hellos' to the masses and accepting the obligatory cup of tea from Katla, Sion waited impatiently for an update. The chatter was relentless and he was finding it impossible to get a word in to any conversation. Finally, after an unsubtle walk around the hoards of cave dwellers, he successfully joined Terry, who was having a high-spirited chat with a man Sion had not met before. Short (obviously) with tight blonde curls, scraped back in a bunch, a piercing in his nose and turquoise overalls. Sion was unsure if he was going to be able to take this man seriously. Some of these cave dwellers certainly had a curious sense of style.

"Hi! Sion! Great to see you! Syd, this is Sion. Lad who 'elped Quinny get the sword back. How are you? Sleep much?"

Syd looked up at Sion and held out his hand. Sion shook it, but was then taken by surprise as he was thrust into a hug.

"Such an honour to meet you, Sion!" Syd began. "What an asset you have become to us. We'd never have the sword back without you. You're a hero!

"Well, I don't know about that. But, thanks. Is it back in a safe place now?" Sion was still desperate to find out what had happened after he'd left Tarquin the previous evening.

"Oh yes! I've forged an especially strong bolt and lock for that one now. Been at it all night. That's why I'm still in these," he gestured at his clothing, with his mug-free hand. "Like I said though Sion, you're a hero to us. So don't you forget it. We certainly won't!"

At this, Syd got up onto a dining chair and shouted the attention of the room. Sion scanned around. There must have been at least thirty to forty people in Geoff and Katla's living room. Granted, most of them were petite in stature, but still, it was a squeeze and it took Syd longer than he wanted to get every eye on him.

"I know we're all only drinking tea, but I'd like you all to join me in giving thanks to our mate Sion here!" He held his filthy hand out above Sion's head. "Three cheers for Sion! Hip hip!" The cheering was deafening and slightly humiliating, despite it being for a good reason. Sion wasn't really into praise and it felt like the three cheers lasted for hours. Syd then issued the same praise for Tarquin, who seemed much more comfortable with the attention. Lapping up the beaming smiles and cheers with a bow and multiple waves to the room. At this point, while the focus was not on him, Sion made his way through the crowd and over to Tarquin.

"Tarquin. You ok? Everything work out fine after I'd gone?"

"Absolutely. Sword is back in its rightful home. Couldn't 'av done it without yer, you know. You were amazing. How you stayed still in the garage, I'll never know. How yer feelin' today?"

"Good. Glad I popped up. So, Bijou? Where do you think she's gone? Surely she'll have to go back to the house. But then what?" Sion gazed up at Tarquin, who was staring up at the ceiling. Which was only a matter of centimetres from his head.

"Goodness knows, Sion. It'll be interestin' to see if she turns up at yer school next week. Can't see it meself. What you thinkin'? Think she'll be there?"

"Nah," Sion replied, "She'll have gone somewhere. I can't see her turning up at school like nothing's happened. Even if she's confident that no one there knows what she's done. Maybe you should drive by the house, see if there's any sign. What do you think?" Tarquin scratched his head and bent down to put his mug onto Katla's tray, as she passed on her way to the kitchen.

"Might be an idea, Sion. We need to be careful though. Wouldn't want anyone thinkin' we're up to anythin'. If they saw us before, I mean. When do you think we should go?"

"Well," Sion began, "If she's not back at school on Monday, how about I message you and we pop over there on Tuesday after school. I'll tell my mum not to come and get me. She's always later on Tuesday anyway. Sound good?"

"Ideal Sion. Right, I need to be off, got work to do. Proper work. Not drivin' about lookin' for stolen artefacts and returnin' them to small people in caves. Proper job work. See yer'on Tuesday, Sion?"

"Tuesday," Sion replied as Tarquin headed towards the door, lifting one hand in acknowledgement. That was Sion's cue to head off too. The atmosphere was electric in that room and it seemed right to leave the cave dwellers to their day of celebrating, before anyone else fancied making him the centre of attention! Sion said a quick farewell to Terry and Geoff. Katla was nowhere to be seen, but was almost certainly busy with something in the kitchen. As he turned to leave, Syd stopped him in his tracks with a hand on his shoulder. Sion saw immediately that he'd changed out of his overalls and was now sporting skin-tight jeans and a strategically ripped, black Megadeth t-shirt.

"Great to meet you today Sion," Syd began. He was eloquent and well spoken, not at all like the other cave dwellers Sion had met, who all seemed to have regional accents of varying locations. It had not been so obvious earlier, when the noise level had been higher. "Look forward to seeing you again some time." He held his hand out once more for Sion to shake, which he did. He was a very curious character, whom Sion wanted to find out more about, but now was not the time.

"Good to meet you too, Syd. I'll be back, I promise." As to not be caught by anyone else, Sion bid Syd farewell and left hastily. On his way home, he realised that in the bustle and chaos of the visit, he'd forgotten to ask about Albert. It could wait. Next on the itinerary was Bijou.

Chapter 37

Where Has She Gone Now?

A Monday morning with RE first lesson, was not usually something to look forward to, but this week, Sion could not be more filled with anticipation. He was certain that she would not be there, but there was always that chance. A double bluff of sorts, she'd act like nothing was going on and continue her teaching as normal. As he arrived at school, Bijou's car was not in the car park. But this meant nothing. She was frequently later than the majority of pupils; waltzing in as the bell went. Sion struggled to maintain conversations with friends, so busy was his mind. Occasionally managing to answer a question about the weekend or about the scores from the Premier League. Never had he been so disinterested in the football scores. It wasn't that he didn't care if Liverpool had won or not, but the results had been pushed back in his priorities by events with Tarquin et al.

As the bell went for their first lesson, Sion ensured that he was the first out of his registration room and headed briskly down the corridor towards Bijou's room. He could see the open door from a distance, walking as quickly as he could without actually breaking into a run. He didn't want anyone to think that he wanted to go to RE!

Turning sharply right into the room, his bag clattering the glass pane, Sion's question was answered. Standing in front of him, looking slightly startled by his rather ungainly entrance, was a tall lady with long black hair held up in a messy bun. Her lanyard distracted Sion from her appearance. No photo. Just the school logo and 'visitor' in large red letters. The lanyard worn by supply teachers.

"Bore da. I'm Miss Evans and you are?" She was a very beautiful lady and Sion was now finding it hard to speak coherently. As he gazed at her, Bijou fell further and further from his mind. Other members of the class were now streaming in and Miss Evans' appearance had seemingly taken them all by surprise. Not only was 'Mrs Anderson' missing, but she'd been replaced by a polar-opposite, in human form.

"I'm Sion. Sion Roberts. Nice to meet you." Sion hurried to his seat, slightly red faced. A silence fell on the room.

"Bore da pawb. My name is Miss Evans and I will be taking your RE classes until the end of the year." There was a low mumbling of gratification coming from all areas of the room. Sion's arm was nudged by Morgan, who said something about being taught by a supermodel. It was then that Sion remembered about Bijou. She hadn't come back. He decided that at the end of the lesson, he must remember to ask Miss Evans if she knew anything of Mrs Anderson's whereabouts.

To say that Mrs Evans was an improvement, as far as RE teachers go, was an understatement of vast proportion. She had a quiz to start, with a forfeit for incorrect answers, she'd managed to book the IPad trolley and she put music on while they were working. Even better than that, it was a Kings of Leon album that Sion's parents had in the car. Sion doubted that all her lessons would be this engaging, but still, she was going to be a lot more tolerable than Bijou and they might actually learn some interesting information.

To his relief, Sion remembered to speak to Miss Evans at the end. As the others shuffled out, he took his chance and stood by the desk to gain her attention, as she turned off the tablets and loaded them back onto the trolley. "Miss Evans, may I ask you a question?"

"Certainly Sion. What's the problem?" Slightly put off by the fact she'd remembered his name already, Sion hesitated slightly, before replying.

"I just wondered if you knew what had happened to Mrs Anderson? We didn't know she wouldn't be here anymore. Is she poorly?" Sion knew this not to be the case, but wondered what on Earth Bijou could've given for a reason to leave so suddenly. He was also fairly sure that even if Miss Evans did know, she wasn't going to disclose private information about another teacher.

"To be honest with you, I'm not entirely sure myself Sion. Obviously, I know I've been asked to stay here until the end of the academic year, but I don't know if she'll be back after that. Sorry to be vague. Did you enjoy today's lesson?"

"Oh yes, it was great. No problem. Thanks for that." Sion hurried out before he sounded anymore ridiculous and before his face turned red for a second time.

So that was that. She'd gone. It was great news as far as RE was concerned, but still a mystery. Even with the sword back inside the cave, it was vital to find out where Bijou was. She'd be angry and wanting revenge and as Sion knew only too well, she wasn't afraid to use violence to get her way. If her home was unoccupied too, then goodness knows where they'd go next. There must be someone Sion could speak to, to find out something, anything. The school must have been given a story, not the real one, but something. Miss Evans was well prepared, she clearly knew about her position before that morning. Sion cursed himself for not thinking of this before. He could've asked her when she'd found out about the job. Or would that've seemed too nosey? She might not have answered him anyway. Sion doubted that Miss Evans did know anything about Mrs Anderson. He may as well, sit back and enjoy her lessons. He'd need to ask someone else in school, if he was going to get anything more substantial. Once they'd been to see Bijou's bungalow, he could ask the headteacher, subtly of course.

Tarquin had obviously been ready and waiting for Sion's email, as he replied almost immediately with confirmation for a visit to Bijou's home the following afternoon. They'd just drive up, take a quick look from the road and go. No hanging about or leaving the van. Sion confirmed he'd be ready after school, in the bus shelter.

And so he was, but Tarquin was late. After the majority of school traffic and bodies had cleared, Tarquin's van emerged, at speed, from the end of the road. "Sorry about that Sion. Got caught up at work. School go well? Any new information?" Sion hauled himself into the passenger seat, moving the magazine onto the dashboard, which Tarquin quickly snatched and stuffed under his seat. Much to Sion's amusement.

"Yeah. School fine. Nothing new though. I'll try to catch the head teacher this week and ask him, but I'll need to think of a reason first. It would be a bit strange for a pupil to be after details of a teacher's private life."

Within three hundred metres of Bijou's house, Sion and Tarquin had their first answer. A 'for sale' sign stood in the front garden of the bungalow. Tarquin stopped the van opposite and both of them stared in silence at Bijou's home. "Looks empty," Sion said.

"Yup. Certainly does," Tarquin agreed. The grass had grown significantly, the drive was empty and the curtains were drawn on one of the windows. Tarquin reached down to the passenger side footwell and emerged with a glossy advertisement for a local supermarket.

"Here," he held the paper towards Sion, "Take this and post it through the letterbox. Try and get a look inside a window, if you can. See if there's any furniture or signs of life." Sion took the paper and climbed out of the van. He wasn't entirely sure that he wanted to go snooping around the bungalow again, but he had to admit, he'd look less suspicious than Tarquin, who, to a stranger, could be likened to a slightly dodgy bailiff.

As he drew nearer, the bungalow seemed increasingly deserted. In the short time that had passed, the seeming lack of human movement had given free rein to weeds and spiders, who'd already begun to take over the path and driveway. Peering through the un-curtained window, Sion felt a shudder of anxiety run through him, as he recalled the time he'd spent, desperate to escape and his silent cowering in the garage. There was no light from inside, the doors he could make out were all closed and all was silent. Behind the distorted glass of the front door, there was a small pile of uncollected post and papers. Sion pushed the letterbox open and glanced inside, before stuffing another useless bit of junk through and onto the pile. Nothing. Not a sound. Just gloom and a musty, vacant smell.

So that was that. What next? Sion and Tarquin did not speak much on the journey back to Sion's house. Clearly, they were both mulling over the same thoughts. Where would she go? With no family above ground and a seemingly small friendship circle, the possibilities were not going to be obvious. Personally, Sion thought that it was unlikely that Bijou would consider any further attempt at reclaiming the sword. She'd know that it'd be more secure than ever and that anyone who's anyone in the caves would know her, no matter how well she tried to conceal herself. "I don't think she'll try again, Sion. What d'you reckon?" Tarquin asked, just as Sion had been considering the same thought.

"No. Surely it'd be too risky for her. She's probably gone a long way from here now. Maybe it'll have been the last anyone will see of her."

"I don't know about that, but I don't think she'll be back any time soon. Not for the sword anyway. She'll be long gone by now, is my guess. Right you are Siony. I'll be in touch. Message any time and remember you're welcome at Geoff's whenever you fancy." Tarquin departed along the lane, leaving Sion standing, staring up at the cave, recollecting the encounter with Bijou. It all seemed so long ago now. So much had happened since his move to the new house. It seemed ridiculous now, to think that he'd been concerned that he'd be bored here. Almost every day had been an adventure and of the most surreal sort. The only negative had been that he couldn't share the excitement of it all with others. And he mustn't. He knew that.

"Who was that dropping you off, Sion?" His mother asked as she appeared from the front door. Sion had been deep in thought and was startled by her sudden arrival. "Sorry Sion, didn't mean to make you jump. Who was that in the van?"

"Tarquin. That removal guy. He lives nearby. He's dropped me off a few times, if he's passing. Quite handy. Especially when the weather has been a bit Welsh. What for dinner?"

"Didn't know he was from around here. He doesn't sound local. Fair enough. He was a nice chap. Very helpful and careful with our belongings. Oh, I did a curry in the slow cooker this morning. That beef and aubergine one. That ok?"

"Yes, definitely. Perfect. You've gone easy on that paste though, haven't you? Nearly blew our heads off last time!" Sion followed his mother and the wonderful scent of red Thai curry paste, inside and closed the door on what had been, another extraordinary and thought provoking day.

Chapter 38

How Does Life Just Move On?

Christmas and New Year seemed like aeons ago. Soon it'd be a year since Sion had arrived here. It seemed ridiculous now that he'd been convinced that life would be dull. Weeks, months in fact, had passed since the triumphant return of the sword. Sion had heard very little from Tarquin and had not visited Geoff at all. School work had increased, the school's football team had been involved in several tournaments and Sion had another interest in his life. An interest in the form of Elin. Elin was in most of Sion's classes and had caught his attention during a football match. Her free kick taking was up there with Lionel Messi. Well nearly. Most of Sion's footballing peers were embarrassed by her talent surpassing theirs. Especially during an inter-school crossbar challenge competition. Sion however, was mesmerised. The only downside was Gwen; dancing about in front of him, daily, singing made up jiggles. Mostly containing the lyrics, 'Sion's got a girlfriend' or 'Sion and Elin sitting in a tree' etc etc.

The Easter break had been glorious. Plenty of sunshine and temperatures pushing 25°C. On the final Saturday, before returning to school, Elin had come over to Sion's to meet his family and go for a picnic. Gwen had hankered for an invite, but it was refused. Much to Sion's relief. He'd decided that Elin was going to visit the cave. Not past The Drop, but just inside. They'd have their walk and picnic around the hill, look at the view across to the sea and then on the way back, he'd show her the cave. As much as he wanted to share some of his knowledge and as wonderful as he considered Elin to be, he mustn't reveal any of that. Yet.

Sion's mum had prepared a picnic. She was in her element, as Elin was a vegetarian and not at all fussy. She'd made falafel, dips and a salad, which contained all manner of things that Sion had never even seen before. Elin identified everything and said that the falafel were the best she'd ever eaten. If she were here, Sion would have given his mum a big hug and kiss for her phenomenal picnic work! He had to admit, it was all delicious and had definitely not impacted negatively on his relationship chances with Elin.

They strolled side by side around the hill, stopping twice to take in the view and watch buzzards. Some fifty metres from the cave, Elin's hand met Sion's. He gripped it tightly. His heart felt like it would burst. She stopped, took hold of his face and kissed him. Only for a second, but that was sufficient for Sion. Now he really knew what was meant by 'butterflies in your stomach'. He was so overcome with the moment, he almost forgot about the cave. That was until it was right there, next to them. Elin spoke first, "Ooo, look! A cave! I love caves. Shall we have a look?"

"Yeah sure, been in a few times. It's very damp and dark and I think there's quite a drop somewhere, so I've heard." Sion tried hard, not to sound too knowledgeable about their location.

"I love that damp, cave smell. I bet the water is so fresh and clean. Running through the rocks and into here," Elin cupped her hand to catch a drip, before licking it from her fingers. "God it's cold!"

Sion knew this. Having fallen into it previously. He shuddered at the memory of it.

Elin heard it first. Talking. Then silence. "Who's that?" Elin whispered, taking hold of his arm.

"That you Sion?" Came a familiar voice from beyond The Drop.

"Yes. I've got a friend with me; we were just having a picnic," Sion replied, while trying not to make eye contact with Elin. Questions were going to come. A lot of questions. His main concern was to ensure that nothing was said that shouldn't be said.

"Who on Earth is that? And where are they?" Elin now sounded anxious and was pulling gently on Sion's arm.

"Don't worry. Just a friend of mine who likes caving. Met him up here a few times. You ok Tarquin?" Sion was hoping that the information about a friend being there had been taken in and Tarquin wouldn't say something he shouldn't. "Found anything today?"

"No, not today. Just having a brew on a ledge. You'll have to join me one day. Find all sorts down here!" Sion sniggered slightly and beckoned Elin to go.

"See you again. We're just off now. Be careful in here, won't you?"

"As always. See you soon, I hope."

Presumably Tarquin was talking to Geoff. Sion's thoughts returned, for the first time in a few weeks, to Bijou. It was funny to think that Elin knew Mrs Anderson as her RE teacher too, but was clueless about her real identity and why she was no longer at school. Surely there'd be news soon. She must be somewhere.

"How do we get down, Sion?" Elin was gazing down towards his house, testing the loose ground with her trainer.

"Down here. See the line in the grass? It takes us to the kissing gate. Gate. The gate," Sion's face reddened again and he avoided Elin's gaze, while simultaneously cursing himself for it. To make amends, Sion took hold of her hand once more and they walked side by side, in a comfortable silence, to the gate. Sion let Elin through first, forgetting his previous gate related comment. Elin went through, turned quickly and landed another kiss onto Sion's crimson cheek.

"You did say kissing gate!" Elin sniggered, as she led Sion through to join her. Looking up at the landing window, Sion could see Gwen pulling faces at them. She'd clearly seen Elin's gesture of affection and he was going to get grief for some time. He didn't care though. It was totally worth it. It had been a perfect day with the perfect company. "Oh look! Your friend is there, coming out from his caving!" Elin pointed up towards the cave, where sure enough, Tarquin was standing, still looking in. Elin put her finger and thumb in her mouth and let out a deafening whistle. Tarquin turned and looked in their direction. Sion waved to him, with his ears still ringing. Elin was blissfully unaware, but Sion knew Tarquin had been talking to someone. Maybe there have been developments. Maybe someone knows something. Maybe she's been found or seen. "It's beautiful here, Sion," Elin wistfully spoke, as she took in the surroundings. "You're so lucky to have this. The peace and quiet." Sion smirked slightly, considering the irony of her statement, following the loudest whistle he'd ever heard and the hustle and bustle of the caves below the hill.

"Yes," he agreed. "It is special here. Cut off from everything; in a way, but I like that." Gwen had joined them on the drive and was chanting her song about kissing, once more. Sion was relieved that Elin chose to ignore this, which he did too. The lack of attention worked and Gwen returned to the house. Sion and Elin smiled at one another. A little victory.

Elin's parents owned a red and black VW Transporter, which Sion drooled over, as it pulled onto the gravel at just after five o'clock. Albert was also intrigued, as Elin's wolfhound Gelert had come for the ride. Gelert and Albert did a few laps of the garden, before returning to the gravel for a sniffathon. "Glad we don't greet each other that way, hey Sion?" Elin's father reached out to shake his hand, which Sion accepted.

"Absolutely!" Sion agreed, "Go on Albert, in! Good lad." Albert retreated to the doorstep and Gelert to the middle seat of the van. "Love your van, Mr Thomas!"

"Call me Dyl! Everyone else does. Yeah, thanks. We sprayed her last summer. Was blue when we bought it, but couldn't stand a blue van, could I? It'd clash with the football shirt and the rugby one for that matter!" Sion was looking for clues to confirm that the team was Liverpool and not United, eventually noticing an LFC car sticker on one of the rear windows. Relief. Even though it might seem ridiculous, if he'd been a United fan, Sion would've found it harder to take to him.

Elin left in the van with Dyl and Gelert, just after six o'clock, in the end. Sion's parents had joined the chat, which had moved on to house renovation talk. While he waited for dinner, Sion went to check his emails. Sure enough, Tarquin had messaged.

Hi Sion,

Good to see your face. Sorry I've been out of the loop, I've not had anything to report until now. Presumably you've not said anything to your friend, but I'm sure you wouldn't do that. Terry found Bijou's car yesterday. It's by woods, at the beach. No sign of her, but the car has been noticed by the police too. It's got a warning on to be removed within the next week, so presumably, it's been there a while. If you fancy a trip out, I'm going down there for a walk around, on Wednesday afternoon, around four. I can drop you home afterwards. Let me know ASAP,

T

Sion hastily replied, agreeing to come. This had been his first excitement linked to the whole saga in weeks! He was going to have to miss football though, which meant missing Elin, but he'd see her the following day. Wednesday's home-time bell could not come soon enough.

Chapter 39

How Will This End?

Tarquin was waiting for Sion, on this occasion. His van had been cleaned too. Not much was said during the fifteen minute drive to the beach car park, until they pulled up. "Car's been towed, by the way. Not sure which day, but it had gone this morning," Tarquin reached under his seat and pulled out a pair of binoculars, "I'll bring these, eh? Might come in handy."

The beach was deserted, bar one elderly gentleman with a terrier type dog, who was tearing up and down the dunes with a stick that dwarfed its tiny fury frame. Tarquin ushered Sion in the direction of the trees, which lined the beach and dunes. A forest of mainly pine. Home to red squirrels, which Sion was yet to see. Despite the clear skies, the forest was gloomy. Eerily quiet. Nothing but bird noise, rustling branches, distant waves and their own footsteps. They both jumped, as a trail runner seemingly appeared from nowhere onto the path in front of them. The tattooed and tanned lady, dressed in fluorescent pink shorts and vest, disappeared into the trees again, further along the path. Once in a while, Tarquin would stop, lift his binoculars up to his eyes and look at nothing. Well, it'd be something, but Sion couldn't see it. Tarquin would then mutter to himself. Conversation was limited, which was unusual, but it wasn't uncomfortable. The quiet was pleasant. The swaying trees, almost symmetrical in their form, framed the path perfectly. The ground underfoot was a mixture of sand and pine needles covering an invisible layer of concrete. Every now and again, a smaller track would branch off to the right, deeper into the forest. The pine trees were dominant, but occasionally, Sion would see an oak or sycamore, which looked completely out of place, with sand around their trunks and roots. On one mighty sycamore, someone had attached a rope with a stick seat. He managed to contain the urge to go and become Tarzan, but made a mental note for future visits.

In the distance, Sion spotted the trail runner again. A flash of pink darting across the path and into the trees once more.

After a good thirty minutes of walking, they came to a break in the trees, which in turn became a picture-postcard outlook. Sand, rocks, sea and a distant horizon. "This is where there was another vent, Sion," Tarquin pointed to a gap in the rocks, next to a sand blasted tree stump. "Not in use now, of course." They sat down on the rocks, facing the sea and Tarquin produced a Mars Bar from his pocket. He broke it in half and handed Sion a piece.

"Thanks," Sion said. He hadn't realised how hungry he was until he saw it. They sat and ate in silence, with just the distant water as white noise. The tide was coming in, but they were in no danger. It rarely came to the top of the rocks, unless there was a storm or a very high tide. Or both. The twinkling, crystal water began to lap at the edge of the salient stone, closest to the sea. Tarquin had seen Sion's pensive look.

"Good for the soul, isn't it?" Tarquin closed his eyes briefly and took a deep breath in through his nose, which made the whiskers above his lip rise upwards. Sion nodded in agreement, not that Tarquin would've seen. He closed his own eyes briefly, to fully absorb the sound of the water. He'd only had a canal and a stream, or brook as the locals called it, near his home in England. He could appreciate that it was pretty, but it was nothing like this. The mighty sea, stretching out in front of you. If you walked in a straight line, you'd be in New York, or maybe Ireland. But still. And the colour too. It wasn't a murky brown, like canal water. It was glittering turquoise with small, ivory waves and silver streaks, where the sunlight caught it. He wasn't keen on swimming, but Sion felt an urge to jump in and submerge himself in the salty breakers.

It was just as he swallowed his last bite that Sion asked Tarquin for the binoculars. "Is that a seal?" he said excitedly, pointing out past the end of the rock mass. Tarquin stood and squinted out towards the dark shape and then snatched the binoculars from Sion, which were around his neck by the leather strap. Sion lurched sideways and managed to un-noose himself. Tarquin continued to look. The more he focussed, the clearer it was that this was not a seal. Its only movement was caused by the sea. Without warning, Tarquin launched himself onto the rocks and began leaping down the small peninsular, towards the sea. Sion followed; a little more wary of the loose ground and slippery stone.

The smell hit them before they reached it. Tarquin, buried his nose into his t-shirt and Sion covered his with one hand, sensibly keeping the other one for balance. As a small wave softly splashed the rocks in front of them, the shape rolled in the surf and bounced gently against the limpet-covered edge. Sion gasped and let out a whine. Tarquin said nothing.

Bijou. Mrs Anderson. Whoever she was. She was cloaked and bruised and most definitely dead. And Sion was sure that she had been the latter for some time. She definitely had not been that colour the last time he saw her. He retched, as Tarquin hauled the body from the sea. "What are we going to do with her?" Sion tried to ask through his hand. Tarquin sat back onto the ground and stared at Bijou's lifeless corpse, which he'd thankfully turned onto its front.

"Well, I think it'd be best to call the police, Sion. Otherwise, we could get ourselves into bother and we don't want that. You got yer phone on you? Mine's in the van." Sion handed Tarquin the phone.

"You do it, I'd not know what to say. Please."

Tarquin got up and walked just out of hearing range for Sion, before returning a few minutes later.

"They're coming now," Tarquin said as he sat back down. "There'll be an ambulance too, to take 'er away. We'll 'ave to stay 'ere and speak to them, obviously."

Sion had never seen a body before, which obviously wasn't unusual for a teenager. He couldn't take his eyes off it. It was like he was expecting her to open her eyes, get up and start knitting, like nothing had happened.

Thankfully for Sion, the police came quickly. They were grateful for his identification of the body, as Mrs Anderson too. He explained about her being a teacher and how she hadn't been in school recently. He and Tarquin gave their statements and that was that. Out of their hands. Bijou was no more. They said their goodbyes to WPO Williams and headed back towards the forest track. As Sion turned for a final time, before the trees engulfed them, he saw the now-bagged body being lifted into the ambulance. He thought about what she'd been doing to get dragged out into the sea. Maybe trying to access the vent. That was most likely. He didn't discuss it with Tarquin at all on the way home. Once again, they travelled in silence, until reaching their destination. Sion jumped out and reached for his bag. "See yer'on," Tarquin said, as Sion was closing the door. "I'll be in touch soon." He hollered as he waved through his open window, honked the van's horn and drove away up the lane. Had Sion known that that was the last time he'd see Tarquin, he'd have shown more enthusiasm. But we rarely know these events are coming, until they hit us head on ...